D. M. Greenwood has worked for thirteen years in the Diocese of Rochester as an ecclesiastical civil servant. Her first degree was in Classics at Oxford and, as a mature student, she took a second degree in Theology at London University. She has also taught at a number of schools, including St Paul's Girls' School in London. She lives overlooking the Thames in Greenwich, with her lurcher bitch.

Heavenly Vices

D. M. Greenwood

HEADLINE

First published in 1997
by HEADLINE BOOK PUBLISHING

First published in paperback in 1997
by HEADLINE BOOK PUBLISHING

10 9 8 7 6 5 4 3 2 1

ISBN 0 7472 5433 8

Printed and bound in Great Britain by
Clays Ltd, St Ives plc

HEADLINE BOOK PUBLISHING
A division of Hodder Headline PLC
338 Euston Road
London NW1 3BH

For Margaret Withers

Contents

CHAPTER ONE

Gracemount

'I've wished him dead many and many a time.'

'Who hasn't? You mustn't blame yourself for that.'

'He did so *much* damage. The college... as Warden...' The Reverend Matthew Brink gestured in his actorly way at the tall French window of his drawing room. Rain battered the glass and bounced off the stone paving of the terrace beyond; each massive drop created its own small fountain. The summer had been dry. Autumn promised a relief.

'I mean,' Brink pressed on, 'Gracemount has always held its head up among theological colleges. It had a certain decorum. The bishops knew their young men were in safe hands here.'

'His wife, his son, are, I suppose, more to be pitied.'

Brink peered across at his companion. The room had darkened with the storm and though it was still early afternoon the latter's features were a smudge in the fading light; his thin figure was lost in the shadow of the leather armchair. Timothy Wade was his senior by several years and though he was a scholar, not in orders, yet Brink, the priest, relied on him, sought his opinion, had wanted, since their university days thirty years ago, to stand well with him. Sometimes Brink felt so inferior to him that he exaggerated his own vivid colours, his energetic style, in order to draw the older man on. In this way he sought validation for his own views, a secular blessing.

'It's left an awful gap in the community. I think we all feel that.' He looked at Wade for confirmation. 'But it's also, don't you feel, a tremendous relief?'

Wade reflected on the character of the late Warden. 'He had a talent for generating tensions.'

'That's it. That's exactly right. He wasn't a peacemaker.' Brink was relieved to have this assurance. 'His stuff,' he went on, 'his papers and the college's files, is in the most incredible mess.' Brink's breathy, enthusiastic voice was defensive, as though he might be blamed for Conrad Duff's lack of order. His upper lip was too short to cover his front teeth and this gave him a questing air. His eyes behind his large glasses were smudged and ill defined as though watery with tears.

Wade perhaps nodded. It was too dark for Brink to be sure.

'You know he made me his executor, his literary executor.'

Wade gazed at the raindrops making runnels down the dusty glass of the windowpanes. Couldn't they afford a window cleaner? He moved his attention deliberately back to his friend. Was Brink proud of his office or resentful? he wondered. 'I didn't know he had anything to be a literary executor of.'

Brink laughed a deprecating laugh which sounded

like a rerouted cough. 'He had rather tailed off recently. I suppose his health . . . But there was always his great vision thing on the Church in the world.'

'*The Darkened Glass.*' Wade was ironic. 'A sort of modern version of Newcome's *Cities of Men, City of God*. Yes? Difficult to see how something like that could be other than a set of generalisations and therefore necessarily superficial.'

Brink thought how much he'd admired Conrad's ability to relate religion to politics. How very clever he had thought Conrad for as long as he'd known him.

'How about the journalism, the occasional pieces?' Wade was a scholar. He didn't hold with journalism. His own publications were solid contributions to his field, efficiently regular and brought out by his university's press. He could afford to be ironic. 'Might there be a slim volume there, if Conrad wants, wanted, a memorial?'

'The difficulty is,' Brink chewed his underlip, 'it's all very much of the moment and there's really no common thread. It would need a lot of editing.'

'Ephemeral,' Wade agreed. Privately he thought Conrad Duff's eye for the currently fashionable and his agility in nipping aboard bandwagons was, if not actually deceitful, at least vulgar.

'I rather thought from something Richeldis said that he'd recently started working on something more,' Brink sought for his word, '*urgent*.' His tone suggested he might be testing Wade out to see what he knew.

'Would she have known?' Wade didn't sound interested. From anyone else, indeed, the question might have been derisory but with Wade, Brink wasn't sure. The late Warden's wife had lived on the periphery of her husband's life for a number of years. They were not separated but they were not together either.

'I suppose not. But why should she mention it, if Conrad wasn't working at something?'

'To tease him, might it be? She knew how much he wanted to count, to have a national voice. Might she have·tormented him by pretending to all and sundry he was engaged on some magnum opus which would have brought in all the public goodies he craved?'

'I suppose that is rather her style. Well, at least she's free of him now.'

For some minutes Wade had been aware of a steady plopping sound behind his left ear. He half turned in its direction. Brink followed his gaze. 'I'll get the bucket.' He padded on slippered feet out into the hall. There was a sound of clanking metal and he reappeared with the sort of bucket that is usually accompanied by a mop.

'It's full, curse it.' He looked round helplessly while the heavy container slopped its contents towards the floor.

Wade rose from his shadowed chair and fiddled with the catch of the French window. He hit it smartly above and below the lock and it lurched open. The wind gusted in bringing wet leaves and rain. Brink seemed still unsure of what was demanded of him. 'Empty it outside,' Wade suggested.

He followed the younger man on to the terrace and watched as he tilted the ungainly vessel towards the gutter below the balustrade. Behind them rose the Gothic revival turrets and pinnacles of Bishop's House, the main administrative block of the college, built over a century ago to accommodate a dozen young men who had chosen to live together to read for Anglican orders. The rain had saturated the Cotswold stone and turned it to a slaty green which, in the respite between showers, glistened, Wade thought, like sweat on a sick man's brow.

For a moment the two men paused and gazed together down the valley towards the rest of the college. An occasional light in the residential quarters, Newcome House, indicated the return for the new term of at least some of the students. At right angles could be glimpsed the dark slate roof of the stables, now a chapel, refectory and teaching rooms. Beyond the buildings the road wound through the wooded slopes of the Chilterns.

'It could finish the college, you know,' Brink burst out. 'The Commission wants an excuse to close us. There are too many of us. Any bit of scandal would go against us. Terminally.' They had returned to the drawing room and Brink was staring up at the ceiling to find out where the leak was coming from. He tapped his foot impatiently against the pail.

'No one need know that he killed himself.' Wade was judicious, practical.

His response did not satisfy his friend. In his anxiety Brink wanted someone to wring their hands and keen with him. He wanted emotion and plenty of it. 'Oh, it'll get out all right. These things always do.'

Wade wondered how many concealed suicides Brink had been a party to.

'There's Richeldis, for a start.'

'Would his wife want it known that her husband had killed himself?'

'How should I know what that woman wants? She's

barking mad.' Distress made the Subwarden abandon his habitual clerical diction. 'I mean if he wanted to take his own life, why not just do it? Why on earth did he have to write all that stuff about decay and degeneration?'

'It was a surprising letter, certainly. Just a single piece of A4 folded once, lying on his dresser.' As his friend's emotion mounted, so Wade became more controlled. His mind went back to that September afternoon when he'd chanced to come up to the college and found them all gathered round Conrad Duff's deathbed. What had actually happened, he wondered, during those two hours when the Warden was breathing his last? 'Have you destroyed it?'

'I wish I had. I didn't get a chance. I only had time to glance at it before Richeldis got her hands on it.'

'Will she spill the beans?'

'Well, it's a month to the day since he died and she hasn't yet. And at least Dr Spender didn't smell a rat.'

'Wasn't that odd?'

'He's young, in a hurry. He's not as punctilious as his father was.'

Wade interpreted his friend's tone. 'Jacob Spender was one of us, wasn't he? He looked after us all.'

Brink nodded. 'Yes. All the old firm. What Conrad used to call "the Court". Neville's not as thorough as his father by a long chalk. Though perhaps in the circumstances . . .' He trailed off. 'But after all, it *was* the second attack Conrad had had. If it weren't for the letter anyone might have supposed it was natural causes.'

Wade grunted. Here we are, he thought, discussing a priest's suicide and its concealment as though it were something on last night's television. How have we all become so divorced from the world, so habituated to an event which, in its way, cries out for resolution, for absolution? Someone – should it be us? – ought to suffer for Conrad Duff's sin. But, surely, that was irrational. It was Duff's sin, not theirs, wasn't it? Only he could pay for it and, presumably, on Brink's theology, he now was.

'It's such a betrayal of all he lived by, was supposed to live by.' Brink was querulous. 'If senior clergy don't embody the faith they teach, what right have they, we, to form young men for the priesthood?'

The plop of water on to the floor an inch away from the bucket indicated that Brink had not judged the fall of the leaking water aright. Petulantly he moved the pail across the damp polished surface.

'So you're just going to have to wait to see if Richeldis keeps her mouth shut or whether she shops you all.' Wade might have been smiling.

'We shall be living on a knife edge,' Brink agreed, never one to abjure a cliché.

'Not a comfortable position for a new term,' was the most his friend would advance him.

The Reverend Isaiah Ngaio felt cold all the time. He hardly knew whether this was a physical or a mental state. He stared at his suitcase on the sofa which doubled as a bed in the tiny attic at the top of Newcome House. He thought of his first wife who had packed it for him whilst his second wife had cooked his last supper and kept the children out of the way. It was seventy-two hours since he had left his schoolhouse in his native land of Umundi on his journey first to the airport at Nairobi, then to London. Now here he was in England at Gracemount St Sylvester. En route he had sampled every kind of transport. He had started at dawn chugging downstream in a dinghy with his two young cousins looking after an unreliable two-stroke outboard. When it faltered, they rowed. He'd transferred first to a donkey cart and then to a worn-out Leyland bus with 'London Transport' still faintly discernible on its sides. Next he'd strapped himself into a jet seat and then stumbled out at the other end into a taxi which, after much delay in traffic, had debouched him on to a train. This had wandered through the Chilterns for some hours before finally putting him down within walking distance of Gracemount.

The further he journeyed from Umundi the more disembodied he began to feel, as though he had died but gone nowhere. He had never been out of Africa before. He had tried to say his prayers before falling asleep in the aeroplane but found he did not know which language he was praying in, Umundese or English.

He remembered his Bishop's last words to him as he shook his hand and blessed him before the start of his journey. 'Remember, Isaiah,' the bright young man had said. 'You must see your time in the UK as a pilgrimage. There you can learn so much which will help your ministry here and benefit us all when you come back to us. The Warden, Canon Conrad Duff, is an eminent scholar, highly regarded in the Church and indeed in national life. He is a very old friend of mine. You will convey my warmest regards to him, please.'

Ngaio had bowed. The man was after all his Bishop even if he hadn't a grey hair to bless himself with and had no wives at all, was, in fact, in the culture of the land, a mere boy. He could have been my son, Isaiah thought from the height afforded him by his six foot stature, his forty years, his two wives and his three sons.

Isaiah remembered his own father who had worn immaculate white gloves but no shoes as he waited at table in Mr McLean's house. Mr McLean had grown coffee and worshipped God in the 1930s in the foothills of Mount Kilino in western Umundi. He treated his servants and workmen with fatherly concern and desired them to have the benefits of the Christian faith. It had been a day of joy when Isaiah's father had agreed to be baptised. His father had acquiesced, perhaps, to please an employer whom he liked. In private he had kept to some of the old ways. Goat's blood had been spilt, the ancestors were not forgotten. But Isaiah, the first son of his second wife, had been in love with the Faith from his birth. He recognised the Word as though he had known it in the womb. It formed him and framed him. A creator Father who enlightened the dark world through the suffering of his perfect Son and thus let loose upon mankind his beneficient Spirit explained all, inspired all, as far as Isaiah was concerned. He learned his own name meant 'Salvation is from God', and a man of God was what Isaiah had wanted, felt himself, to be.

Mr McLean had paid for him to train as a schoolteacher; later he had been accepted into deacon's orders. There he might have rested. He was without ambition. But then there had arisen the opportunity for two years' study in England with the expectation that thereafter he should be priested. Isaiah had not been the Bishop's first choice but the hand of Providence had moved. The first candidate had taken a fever (AIDS had been hinted at) and had died within a month. The Bishop's eye had lighted upon Isaiah. So, three weeks later, here he was.

The good Bishop is right, Isaiah conceded, I am here to learn, to learn all kinds of things. He felt his heart beat quicker at all there was to learn, like how to unpack a suitcase without a wife on hand, and where and when to eat; above all, how to get warm. In this latter quest Isaiah studied his room. There were a number of choices. For example, tucked into the corner of the attic was a small cast-iron grate. Isaiah squatted down to inspect it more closely. His practical eye took in the possibilities. A cinder box beneath the bars of the grate was in working order. He peered beneath the canopy. There was a cover with a hook in it which would need to be removed before the smoke could find its way up the flue of the chimneypiece. He experimented with pushing it up and then, when it did not yield, sliding it forward and down. With a grinding of iron on iron, it moved. The little metal flap slid out bringing with it a smell of soot and dust.

The Lord was bountiful, for together with the soot came a packet of paper which would do well for kindling. Now all that was needed was a log or two. And had he not passed a pile of logs behind the gatehouse as he came up the drive an hour ago? Doubtless they were placed there for just such a need as his. He would go forth and seek. Pleased with his resource, Isaiah brushed himself down, seized his

umbrella, opened his door and strode down the corridor
in search of the wherewithal for his first home comfort.

Theodora Braithwaite, a woman in her thirties in
deacon's orders in the Church of England, stamped
on her brakes to avoid running down a man attired in
the heavy cotton makshi of a respectable member of
the Umundi middle class. The wide brown and red
skirts scarcely cleared the earth. She had last seen
such a dress when she'd served as a curate in Nairobi
ten years ago and travelled into the neighbouring
territory of Umundi.

The figure raised the umbrella and lowered it in
courteous greeting. It clasped, she saw, a number of
logs under its arm. Through the driving rain Theodora
glimpsed the modelled, regular features she'd admired
in the flesh as well as in the portrait sculpture of the
Umundi craftsmen. Her spirits lifted. It was like a
homecoming finding something so agreeable in the
middle of the Chilterns. Would there be many overseas
students at Gracemount?

As if in response to her own mood the rain suddenly
ceased and the strands of grey cloud parted to reveal
the sun which had been behind them all the time. She
slowed to take the corner and the house stood before
her. The mock Jacobean front porch set off the Victorian
Gothic nicely. She deciphered 'The Lord is My Shep-
herd', modelled in stone letters, now a little out of
alignment, running round the cornice. Ferns grew from
the soil pipe and there was a small buddleia in its
final glowing colour springing from behind the crocket-
ing of the north tower.

'Gracemount's going through a rough patch,' the

vicar of her south London parish of St Sylvester's
Betterhouse, Geoffrey Brighouse, had said as he waved
her off. Well, which of the theological colleges wasn't?
Training priests by secluding them from the world for
two or three years and making them read a lot was
an expensive and perhaps not very efficient way of
forming them for life in the parishes. Was it a doomed
system of education? She thought back to her own
experience of theological college twelve years ago. She'd
gone on after Oxford. She'd moved with relief from
the rigours of the study of the classical world with its
clear, crystalline values and rational, uncharitable
virtues to the totally different world of first-century
Jewish Christianity. She'd enjoyed it, she had to admit.
The rhythm of work and prayer, the opportunity to
concentrate utterly on what was of first importance
evoked her gratitude still. But then she was bookish
and from a clerical family. Eight generations of
Braithwaites had served the Church of England in
one priestly capacity or another. She was, she had
begun to suspect, not quite typical. Perhaps something
more practical, more orientated to the hardness of the
world was needed now.

It was partly driven by such thoughts as these that,
in between her duties as curate at St Sylvester's
Betterhouse, she had started to research the life of
Thomas Henry Newcome, the Victorian divine who
had founded St Sylvester's Gracemount, as well as
her own church in Betterhouse. A Tractarian, much
stirred by the lives and writing of Pusey and Cardinal
Newman, he had used his considerable private fortune
to set up a foundation and religious order dedicated
to supporting and training priests in the catholic

12

tradition for work in city parishes. Part of the archive for his life and work was in London at the Foundation of St Sylvester but part, too, was lodged in Newcome's original home at Gracemount.

Eager for a respite from London and the parish's demands before winter closed in, Theodora contrived a week's leave, borrowed a car, and drove, free as air, down to the college in the Chilterns. As she drove, she allowed herself the luxury of meditating on Newcome. She had hunted him down the nights and down the days of his published works. Newcome, apparently so open and accessible, known to her from his published work, his sermons and scholarly volumes, above all from his greatest book, *Cities of Men, City of God*, had managed so far to elude her as a private person. It was not that she suspected him of deliberately presenting her with a misleading facade, it was merely that the tenor of his life had been built on a public, indeed on a monumental, scale. But the foundations of that monument were hidden. She had little idea of what the domestic Newcome had been like. As a biographer, as a Christian, she was committed to the view that the springs of action, however socially shaped, were formed in the moral passions of the private, the inner life: what had he loved, what had he feared?

Now, at last, at Gracemount, there would be opportunity to look deeper, for here were stored his private papers, his letters and diaries. She felt herself to be closing in on her quarry. She had traced his friendships and family connections through Tractarian society in nineteenth-century England. And if this had not shed all the light she desired then, surely, to tread the paths he trod, to view the gardens which he himself had laid out and stroll along the terrace he knew when he meditated his great work would bring her closer to him. She had lived with him so long now that she ardently wished to meet him, as it were, off the lead, at the moment of composition before the final form of the work had been given. If she could only encounter a palpable ghost and interrogate it, she would be satisfied. Hunter, detective, conjurer, she knew not what she was but she was determined to have a real person to present to the world in her biography, not some lay figure nailed to a rehearsal of his chronological history. She had faith enough in the stature of her hero to feel sure that he would not fail her in this final test of his quality.

Theodora steered carefully round the deep ruts in the drive (the car was not her own) and followed the listing signpost's arm directing her to Newcome House, Refectory, Chapel. She recognised the figure walking towards her before she was herself recognised. She tapped the horn.

'Stephany!'

'Theo! Jamie, come out of the way, sweetie. Henry, come and meet Aunty Theo.'

The Reverend Doctor Stephany Prior greeted the Reverend Theodora Braithwaite. Theodora looked with distaste at the two young, how very young, children strung round her friend. She had hoped to avoid too evident domesticity. Stephany posed, one child in her arms, the other at her side. All three waited to be admired, set against the streaks of red and grey sky with the dark stone of Newcome House in the background. Theodora hardened her heart. She was here for a serious purpose, the pursuit of truth; *mauvaise foi* was to be avoided.

'It's lovely to see you,' she said with genuine warmth, addressing her friend and ignoring her children.

'Say hello, Jamie,' commanded his mother with determination, moving the child in arms in Theodora's direction. The child placed his thumb in his mouth and turned himself back to his mother's shoulder. Theodora smiled warmly at him. Sensible boy.

'Say hello, Henry,' the mother persevered.

'You're very tall,' said the boy on the ground.

'Six foot one,' Theodora agreed. 'How tall are you?'

'I'm one hundred and thirty-three centimetres,' the modern youth responded.

'They seem sensible,' she admitted to Stephany.

'They're both very like Aidan.'

'Who is, I hope, well?'

'Well, being a father and reading for ordination and being married to me as a priest is rather a role conflict situation for him, poor dear.'

'Father, student, husband and ordinand. What an excess of virtue he must have.'

'Well, you know Dan.'

Theodora agreed she did. She'd known him at university where he'd practised marathon running and Greek prose composition. He'd done well. Nothing seemed to be difficult for him. His school, his family, his friends all had the feeling of good quality about them. Aidan had never needed to swagger or boast. Effortlessly he had been a golden boy. Then he'd gone out East for some years and returned with his Australian wife. She'd taken deacon's orders in Australia and then been priested in England as soon after the vote as was possible. Theodora had met up with them again in London where Aidan had worked for a city bank and Stephany had completed her studies. Soon after that Aidan had decided to test his vocation. They and their two children moved down to Gracemount. Because she had a doctorate in sociology, Stephany had no difficulty in securing a teaching post at the college. Sociology was in, as far as the Church of England was concerned, was, indeed, more in than theology. Where did that leave Aidan? Theodora wondered; in his wife's shade perhaps.

'Where do I sign in?'

Stephany gestured towards the block behind her. 'You've got a room up in the attics, I know. But you'd better check with the bursar first. She doesn't like to be bypassed. Her office's in Bishop's House.' She pointed back the way Theodora had driven.

'Give Henry and Jamie and me your bag and we'll take it up, won't we,' she turned her head to each of her children in turn, 'while you go and sign in. You'll come to supper, won't you? Aidan's terribly excited at seeing you again.'

Theodora found it hard to believe this since nothing excited Aidan. Marathon runners don't get excited and Greek prose composition is a low-key activity. Still, if Stephany wanted Aidan to be excited, excited no doubt he would do his best to be.

Theodora started back on foot along the track which she had just driven down. The pools in the unraked gravel reflected the dark shapes of limes and beeches, some of which Newcome must have planted. He had not seen them in their mature glory, which was now. Theodora recalled the passage, in one of Newcome's

letters, about the laying out of the gardens. He had
described how he had created a ride through the woods
halfway down the drive. She paused and glanced left
and right. There it was, a green way three or four
metres wide, fringed with holly and ash. 'Which
terminates,' she recalled his words, 'with the fountain
of Hermes – the gift of my dear wife.' Theodora knew
very little about Henry Newcome's wife, Esther. She
rather assumed she was one of those props to famous
men without whom not, a fit dedicatee for the first
published volume. Mrs Newcome was so far nothing
more than a reference in the footnotes of the letters
of the period, mentioned because she had married a
distinguished man.

Theodora did not hesitate. There could be no resist-
ing the detour. She turned to follow the track as it
rose gently before her. Sun slanted through the trees.
Brown beech leaves clung to the unmown grass. The
grass itself was spongy beneath her shoes.

There was no Hermes. His plinth was there but the
statue itself, which Theodora had so vividly imagined
from Newcome's description, was absent. Only the pool
which had once surrounded him remained. She advanced to the edge of the pool. It was a perfect circle about
six metres across, its white coping stone giving it the
air of a basin, for it stood slightly proud of the turf.
The water was a deep black-green and as Theodora
gazed into its depths she thought she caught a gleam
of silver fish. A flurry of wind presaged the return of
rain and the surface rippled and mantled.

Theodora allowed her eye to travel round the whole
of the pool. Then she stopped. Opposite, with his back
to her, was the figure of a youth about the right age

for a Hermes. He was tall and thin. His running shorts
were skimpy. He looked as though he had not so much
grown as been stretched. He was standing in about
two foot of water at the edge of the pond. For a moment
Theodora wondered if he had risen out of the pond.
Was he entering the water or had he come from it?
His hair was dark with water and plastered in flat
tongues down the side of his bony head.

He must have felt her gaze upon him for he turned
round suddenly, his feet churning mud and water as
they changed position. Water ran down his face and
dripped unchecked from his chin. 'My father's dead.'
His voice was husky as though from long desuetude.

'I'm so sorry. When did that happen?'

The boy looked baffled. 'I don't know. A fortnight.
No, more. A month now.'

'Who was your father?'

'The Warden.'

Theodora recognised the tone this time. It was ironic.
The boy began to shake. His mouth contorted, the
corners turning down like the classical mask of tragedy.
He began to rock to and fro on his heels, making small
rings in the rain-splattered surface of the water.

'I killed him.'

Theodora, though sympathetic, was averse to
hysteria. She thought it sprang from too cultivated
and theatrical an ego, 'Surely not,' she remarked
bracingly.

'I loathed him.' The boy was resentful, and not to
be cheated of his drama.

'Loathing can't kill.'

'Mine can,' said the boy. 'My loathing is deadly.'

CHAPTER TWO

Priestly Formation

'This is Isaiah Ngaio,' said Stephany to Theodora. 'Isaiah, this is Theodora Braithwaite.'

Theodora thought back quickly to the conventions of hand-giving by women in East African society. She gave it. Isaiah took it.

'I am very happy to make your acquaintance,' Theodora led.

'I too am delighted to make your acquaintance. I hope you are in good health.'

'I am in good health. I hope you too are well.'

'Thank you. I am in good health.'

'You have travelled a long way.'

'It is indeed a long journey. I am glad to have arrived safely.'

'You are very welcome to our cold country.'

Isaiah's smile was beatific. Here was someone who knew how a greeting conversation should go, who had a proper sense of things. The woman was clearly well bred. All that had been said would have translated beautifully into his beloved

Umundese. He prepared to continue.

Stephany had had enough. 'Theo spent her first curacy in your neck of the woods.' Her Australian accent was strong in order to assert her identity. Damn it, whose lounge was this?

'Ah, which part of our country?'

'I had two happy years in Nairobi and I travelled about a bit, Umundi to the north and into West Africa. Lagos.'

Ngaio shuddered. 'Lagos, the Babylon. There is violence and great iniquity. I am myself from Umundi.'

'Africa is rougher than England, certainly, or more overt. But I got very attached to it. Some lovely Christian people.'

'They're very warm, aren't they?' Stephany chipped in.

Theodora was disturbed to detect irony in her friend. She must have picked it up at Gracemount, for she had never manifested any trace of it when they had known each other in London. Theodora sprang to protect her new acquaintance. 'Dignified is a word that comes to mind.'

Stephany could see she might lose this one to Theodora so she was glad to hear Aidan's step on the uncarpeted stairs. There was a moment's silence and Theodora could visualise him hesitating before he opened the door on his guests.

'Don't skulk, Dan,' his wife called.

Aidan surveyed the room. His wife insisted on spotlights of tremendous wattage. The room was slashed, therefore, with shafts of brilliant light whilst other bits of it were in deep shadow. The furniture was general issue married quarters. The overall effect was of some year ten carpentry class having had its way with pine planks only casually differentiated into sofa, chairs and table. All articles napped to the horizontal to be at one with the floor, the bright yellow boards of which had been sealed and glossed so that the ethnic rugs slid about on them. Those who knew the room were careful to get their footing right, as though on a ski slope, before moving about. Shielding his eyes against the glare of his wife's theatrical lighting, Aidan identified his wife, a black man and 'Dear Theo', he said, but did not embrace her or shake hands. He smiled his cloudless smile.

'Aidan, what a long time!' She would scarcely have recognised him. He had more than aged. His skin was stretched over the bones of his face in a grey mask. For a moment she felt a tremor of fear.

He continued smiling and turned to Isaiah. 'Mr Ngaio, isn't it?'

'It sure is,' said Stephany, intent on not letting the greeting thing get under way again.

But Isaiah had risen and was embarked. 'I am very happy to make your acquaintance. I hope you are . . .'

'Theo, come and say night-night to Jamie and Henry.'

Theodora, thinking how much rather she would like to witness the greeting ritual, followed her hostess across the treacherous floor to the children's room.

'Hey! How you people do go on.'

'It's the custom. It's thought impolite to rush your fences.'

'Life's too short.'

'Human relations are felt to need a degree of ritualisation, of caution, at least initially.' If she were to oblige

21

her hostess by applauding her children, she would at least give herself the pleasure of theorising.

The children's room was full of blue kangaroos, some stencilled on the walls, some free standing, made of nylon fur. They were not an animal of much character, in Theodora's view, nothing like as evocative as a teddy bear. Would that be because there was no literature to back up the roos or were they dullards by nature? The room smelt of talcum powder. In the shaded night light Theodora discerned two humps in two separate beds. The two boys lay innocent and unmarked. Their heads were fair like their mother's but their expressions, concentrated and remote in sleep as though visiting another land, reminded Theodora of their father.

'Is Aidan . . .' she began.

'You saw.' Stephany rounded on her. Her fair hair was loose and shoulder length. It swung round after she had turned her head. 'He's not well, is he? He looks like death and he's not sleeping. And he won't tell me what's wrong. He keeps, well, evading me. He hasn't run for weeks. Ever since . . .'

'Since?'

'You know the Warden died?'

'It made the nationals as well as the *Church Times*.' Theodora recalled the *Church Times*'s limp headline: 'Sudden Death of Leading Catholic Leaves Gap'. 'Has it made waves?'

'I guess all deaths do that and perhaps ought to. But Dan and Conrad Duff were quite close in a way.'

'Father and son?' Theodora hazarded.

'Something like that. I got the feeling Dan and he had some sort of joint venture in hand recently. He'd seen a fair amount of Conrad after the end of term. But he wouldn't tell me what it was about. Theo, did you know Conrad Duff?'

'No. That is, I never met him. I heard him preach once at Pusey House when I was an undergraduate. He preached on tradition and quoted from the Latin fathers rather too much. It was adroit rather than scholarly, I thought.'

'You mean he was a show-off?'

'It was all very polished.'

'I couldn't make him out. He made a lot of fuss of Dan and me when we first came. But I'm not sure how genuine he was. He seemed very English. A type we don't have down in Aussie. I couldn't tell whether he meant what he said. Was he real or pseud?'

'Pseud?'

'Well, like you say, scholarship displayed to impress rather than illuminate. Matt Brink always reckoned he wanted a bishopric.'

'No good displaying scholarship in that case.' Theodora was tart.

'I don't mind him not being a scholar. I guess I just didn't feel the Gospel led him.'

Theodora realised, as she had done before in her relations with Stephany, that she was a very straightforward Christian. It was almost as though Stephany kept her religion in a separate compartment from the rest of her intellectual pursuits. How could someone so sophisticated about the working of institutions in society be so flat earth about religious beliefs?

'Theo, you've known Dan a long time, longer than me. Yes?'

'I suppose so.'

'If he talks to you . . . He may. I know he trusts you.'

'Then I shall listen,' Theodora said. She certainly wasn't going to promise to pass on any confidences Dan might impart. Surely Stephany must know that. On the other hand she had to admire Stephany's generosity. Not every wife would acknowledge her husband's former friends as possible confidantes. Perhaps it was a measure of Stephany's desperation that she had asked. For a moment Theodora remembered the dripping figure of Duff's son standing in the Hermes pond and felt a frisson of fear. What had been going on at Gracemount? She looked at Stephany's hands as they grasped the newel posts of her elder son's bed. The knuckles showed white.

'How do you come to know Isaiah?' she asked to relieve the tension.

'I don't. I met him on the stairs just after I left you. He looked cold and kind of lonely so I offered supper. He's sweet, isn't he? He's got the attic one down from you. Come on. Let's go and eat. You'll be peckish after that drive.'

Aidan said grace. Pork, lentils, celery and parsnips appeared. The bread was homemade. There was a green salad dressed in walnut oil. The goat's cheese came from the woman in the village who milked her own animals. The wine was a heavy purple Cahors. Stephany was a good hostess, unfussy, liberal, keeping supplies and conversation going at a good pace without strain. But Aidan wasn't doing his share. Like his sons he seemed to be elsewhere.

Isaiah Naigo told them of life in Umundi and his hopes for his course at Gracemount. Aidan ought to have been interested. He wasn't, Theodora remembered, a great performer himself but his strength lay in a good quality of listening, a prompt attentiveness which helped people to articulate old thoughts and expand into new ones without fear. Theodora had sometimes thought that Aidan would, in the end, teach. His wanting to become a priest had surprised her.

Theodora contributed her bit. She wondered as she did so why they needed to say so much. Didn't they trust each other enough to enjoy each other's silence? But she knew enough of Stephany to be sure that any dead spots would be considered a sign of social failure. In the end it was Stephany herself who let the topic of death back in.

'Have you got your induction course sassed, Isaiah?'

Isaiah patted his broad chest arrayed in its brown and red cotton swathe. 'I carry the papers always with me. We start tomorrow with the Holy Eucharist at seven forty-five a.m., then breakfast at eight thirty a.m. Then I am instructed to meet with a Mr Fisher to tour the facilities. Then there is a break for coffee at eleven a.m. Then . . .'

He had clearly committed it to memory, Theodora thought. He'll do his theology course like that, memorising large chunks of what he hopes is relevant material from recommended texts. That was how they did things in Africa.

'Then I have to meet my tutor, the Reverend Brink,' Isaiah was pressing on. 'Then we have lunch at one p.m. Then the Warden addresses us new students at two thirty p.m.'

There was a pause. Aidan's voice was low and difficult to hear. 'I'm afraid we have no Warden at the moment, Isaiah. Canon Duff died at the beginning of the holiday.'

Isaiah made the sign of the cross. 'I am deeply sorry that it should be so. But God's holy will be done.' He paused and then added, having searched his own experience, 'The fever is widespread in the UK?'

'He had a heart condition,' Stephany said.

'But it was sudden,' Theodora offered.

Aidan said quietly, 'He shouldn't have died.'

'Now look here, Dan.' Stephany's accent was prominent again.

Did Isaiah sense tension or an impending indecorum or was he simply following up his own interests? How difficult it was to read all but the most intimate of one's acquaintances. Theodora looked at Isaiah's broad brow and well-defined nose. The planes of his blue-blackness glistened in the peculiar slanting light of the room. Whatever his reason he moved in quickly. 'I regret greatly I shall not be able to convey the warm regards of my Bishop to the late Warden. They were, I understand, old friends. The Warden was a most distinguished scholar, it seems.'

Stephany snorted. 'Depends where you start from, I guess.'

'The Bishop was mistaken?'

'Scholar is a fine word. It shouldn't be devalued by waving it over just any old bod who likes reading books, or indeed writing them.' Aidan was passionate beyond need. 'Scholarship has to do with truthfulness. It's a moral term.'

'Dan means standards aren't high in the good old C of E at the moment, would you say, Isaiah?' Stephany slipped into her tutorial role.

Theodora felt this was a bit unfair. The man hadn't been in England more than twelve hours. Aidan also felt this. 'Unlike those obtaining in sociology, sweetie?'

'We haven't sunk as low as you lot yet.'

'Theodora's biography will be an exception,' Aidan said. 'It will set new standards in biography and historical theology.'

Isaiah was lost. 'I do not understand your remarks,' he said firmly. They were white, of course, and so felt that they knew everything. But they were also women and had, therefore, surely, a different place from men.

'Stephany's research area is sociology of religion. She's on the staff here. She's also in priest's orders. Theodora's in deacon's orders but she's better educated than Stephany owing to Cheltenham Ladies and Oxford.' Aidan filled Isaiah in on the peculiar snobberies of the English scene with something of his old relish. 'She's also writing a biography of Thomas Henry Newcome, the nineteenth-century Tractarian who actually founded Gracemount. You'll find his portrait in the dining hall on the west wall opposite the servery.'

Isaiah saw that there was much to be assimilated here. But felt he'd better put down his own marker. 'In my country women are in deacon's orders only. Not very many of them write books.'

'You'll get used to it, I expect,' Stephany said without rancour. 'And believe me, you're better off with me and Theo than you'd ever be with Conrad Duff.'

'May he rest in peace,' said Isaiah to bring concord.

Conrad Duff who was recently dead, Thomas Newcome who had been dead a century and Aidan Prior who lived yet, though he looked like death, all merged in

Theodora's dream into a single male presence. In her dream she saw the single figure but the triple personality as though she were lodged high up in the clerestory of a chapel looking down on him preaching to a congregation huddled below in the choir. The chapel seemed to be open to the elements, roofless and ruined. The words of the preaching figure came fitfully on the wind, flapping round the pillars like the flapping of the surplices of the boy choristers. She kept straining to hear. It was very important that she should hear what the man was saying. Something terrible would occur if she did not.

Theodora woke in her little attic room to the banging of her casement window and the rattle of rain on dry leaves. For a moment the remnants of the dread which had suffused her dream stayed with her. Then the pleasure of the season and the gift of a whole day, a whole week, to be organised as she wished, dissolved the phantoms. She began to plan. A reconnaissance of the grounds, Eucharist, breakfast and then the library. She would return to the pattern of reading she'd followed as an undergraduate: ten to one, two to five and a couple more hours after supper to organise her notes. She had determined her first task. She needed to clarify the chronology and events of the year immediately prior to the publication of *Cities of Men, City of God* in 1879. The motivation for that extraordinary work, its prescient analysis of industrial society and the Church's relation to it would, she was resolved, become clear to her. Nothing in Newcome's previous writings, his sermons and pamphlets, gave any inkling of the quality of that final work. Here, on his little estate, what was concealed in the life and thought of the first Warden of the college would be laid open.

She lacked only a dog, Theodora thought, as she put her head into the wind and felt the soft rain on her face. A Labrador would have relished the country. It was almost light. Dawn-coloured rabbits were returning to burrows. A hungover-looking fox could scarcely raise his head to glance in her direction. She took the turn from the main drive into the ride and passed the Hermes pond with its empty plinth. Where was the messenger of the gods? she wondered. Thrown down, overturned and languishing in the nettles, its marble stained by grass and moss? Or had it been sold on? Where, too, was the late Warden's son, her encounter of the previous evening? Her instincts were pastoral. The boy was in need; ought she not to seek him out and offer what help she could? She caught herself up. She was on another errand entirely. If her research was any good and her biography of sufficient quality to command attention, it might direct the thoughtful to return to the roots of the catholic revival in the Church of England at a time when that wing of the Church was demoralised. What was it that made such movements possible? Nothing, surely, but the virtuous actions and courage of individuals. And why should not similar giants arise in our own time?

From the distance came the sound of a clock striking seven. She pushed on to the end of the ride. Who would succeed Conrad Duff? There was, of course, no rational connection between her research and the choice of a new Warden but in some way Theodora felt that the wardenship of the theological college with its catholic traditions was bound up with the virtue and reputation of its founder. A worthy successor was needed, for Gracemount was worth preserving, wasn't it?

She emerged from the woods and found herself on the opposite side of Bishop's House with a clear view over the valley. The house, therefore, which looked from the front as though it was set on a plane, was actually perched on the side of a cliff; the ground fell away from this side almost precipitously. Immediately in front of the building the slope had been terraced. Gravelled paths, now rife with couch grass and grounsel, connected the descending levels. The beds, which Mrs Newcome had planted with verbena and heliotrope in whose scent she had rejoiced in the cool of the evening, now yielded only briar and dandelion. But to either side of the house no cultivation had gone on. Rough sheep pasture ran down to the road and the river in the valley. In the distance a horse whinnied and another answered it. Theodora's gaze followed the lines of river and road and made out the turn to the village. There, unmistakable to the trained eye, were the outbuildings of a stable. Temptation rose up. How very pleasant it would be to hack through these beech woods instead of walking around them. Perhaps she might just drop down there early tomorrow morning and see what offered.

For the present, however, she struck off round the remaining unknown side of the house, crossing the strip of gravel and lawn. She peered through the panes of the downstairs rooms.

She had seen a little of Bishop's House yesterday evening. She had wandered through the long dark corridors remarking the dusty panelled wood disfigured

by modern fitments. She observed and regretted the
modernity which had been clumsily affixed to the fabric
of a once handsome building such that the eye was
constantly affronted or disappointed. Neon bar lights
traversed the coffered ceiling of the library. Warped
strips of hardboard blocked the elaborate chimney-
pieces. Plastic and metal tables and chairs were stacked
incongruously in the middle of the well-proportioned
rooms. No eye had cared for harmony, scale or suit-
ability. In rage and haste to obliterate what they did
not understand or value, they had pressed on. No,
surely it wasn't so intentional, just random, piecemeal
response to unplanned needs. By default the house
was despoiled. Theodora was reminded of the recent
revisions of the Church's liturgy. Both spoke of an
institution not at ease with itself, its history or the
modern world.

When at last she had lighted upon the bursar's office,
the bursar had looked at her in amazement and then
handed her a survival kit consisting of a key, a list of
mealtimes and a site map.

'You'll be leaving us . . . when?' the square woman
had asked, putting first things first.

'Saturday,' Theodora had answered. 'Next Saturday.
I asked for a week. Is that all right? When I telephoned
you said—'

'Oh, right, yes, a week. That's fine. It's just that
we've got an influx midweek. A bishop and his archdeacon. They're trustees. They may want to stay the
night, though I do hope not. We're a bit pressed for
rooms. We don't usually use the attics. So some of us
may have to squeeze up a bit. Not you, though. Attics
aren't suitable for trustees. I was hoping we could use

31

the Warden's apartments but Mrs Duff says no way.'
The bursar shook her short grey locks. As though to
compensate for the shortness of the hair she wore a
pair of very long heavy earrings of blue plastic birds
dangling either side of her cheeks and framing her
square face like some ancient headdress.

'Gainley, by the way,' said the bursar, suddenly
thrusting out a hand in Theodora's direction as though
she had come to a conclusion about Theodora's bona
fides. 'Thelma Gainley. We're waiting for the rush.'
Mrs Gainley indicated the piles of folders colour-coded
and stacked on the table.

'How many have you got this year?'

'Twelve,' said Mrs Gainley. 'We lost a couple of first
years from Litchfield when their DDO heard about
the Warden's death.'

'Is that going to be a pattern?' Theodora asked.

'The Lord knows.' Mrs Gainley's tone indicated she
was prayerful rather than profane.

'Conrad Duff was a considerable figure,' Theodora
pressed.

'He knew a lot of people,' Mrs Gainley conceded.
'In all walks of life.'

'Will you survive?'

Mrs Gainley looked reality in the face. 'We're not
on the up and up at the moment, are we? Now, have
you got all you need?'

'Library pass?'

'Mr Spin knows you're coming. I expect he'll be glad
of the company.'

And so they had parted. Theodora, twelve hours
later, peering through the unwashed panes of the
French window, wondered how this little leaderless

community with its decaying grandeur on the edge of
the hills would fare.

CHAPTER THREE

Low Table

'His wife killed him.'

'Not a shred of proof. He died of a heart attack.'

'Richeldis was there. She loathed him. She put the evil eye on him.'

'I loathed him. His son loathed him. He was an odious man, deserving of being loathed.'

Trevor Fisher was very fond of Rita Nougatt. Rita quite liked Trevor. They manifested their affection by constant bickering. They wore identical hand-knitted green and white pullovers done on Trevor's mother knitting machine while she was learning how it worked. They had started their ordination course together a year ago and would finish it in nine months' time. Trevor was helping Rita to unpack books from a tea chest. But he showed his independence by not putting the volumes where she told him to. Thus, amicably, they related. Later she would give him a hand with his stuff in his rather larger room two floors up in Newcome House. Collegiate life was easier in all sorts of ways if you had a reliable mate.

'Still, I don't know.' Trevor felt he had to defend his own sex. 'Of the two of them I reckon Richeldis is the worse. She never talks to you but you feel you've got the wrong pully on. She's patronising.'

'That's how I felt about Conrad Duff. He regretted me being a woman.'

'Could have been just you.'

'Could have been.' Rita was as honest as the day in such matters and never overestimated her charms. Seven years in the Local Authority Services Department in Oldham had left her clear-sighted about every human folly including her own. 'But he did it to all the women.'

'All three of you.'

'Vastly civil, he was, but just somehow, because we weren't chaps . . .'

'He didn't want women priests.'

'If he'd bothered to ask me, I could have set him right on that score. I'm not going to be priested. Deacon'll do for me.'

'Sez you.'

'You doubt me?' Rita swung round on him.

'Nay, nay, hinny,' Trevor mimicked cowering. He had no vocabulary for expressing emotion and so when the need arose, he adopted a sort of music hall dramatisation of northern laddishness. Since he came from Newcastle, southerners sometimes supposed this was the way they talked up there. When he found himself in a position where he could not avoid giving an account of how he had come to want to serve the Church more than he wanted anything else in life, he would say, 'Jesus wants me for a sunbeam.' It took someone of Rita's experience to see he wasn't a fool.

'So what did he die of then?' he asked, not caring.

'Heart.'

'I thought you said he didn't have one.'

Rita swiped at him with a folder. 'Mrs Gainley says Richeldis stopped it for him.'

'How does she know?'

'She never sleeps and she never goes away. She was here all over the vacation.'

'But she can't have been in at the death.'

'No, but Aidan Prior was.'

'He wouldn't make wild statements like that. Very close, Aidan, very. . .' He sought for words.

'Upper class, public school, well bred?' she hazarded from a vocabulary wider than his but based on the concrete and sharing his social values.

'I was going to say thoughtful, priestly even. He'll make a good priest.'

'Depends how much of himself he's willing to put into the common pot. Not a communicator. Not a sharer.'

'No, but he's prayerful. And he's a carer all right. I wouldn't be going through all this lot,' he waved his hand at the piles of books and files, 'with two kids to support and a grant of a couple of thousand a year.'

'They've got Stephany's salary. Oh, and she asked me, would we babysit Sunday night. I said OK. That all right?'

'Suppose so. Did she mention supper?'

'She'll leave something out. Always does. Not mean.'

'No,' he agreed.

'Come on,' she said, imitating his accent. 'Look sharp. We've got time for a cuppa coffee before you pick up your little sponsoree.'

Trevor speeded up his book handling as though he were stacking supermarket shelves. 'And anyway,' he took up the thread of the previous conversation, 'what did Mrs Gainley say Dan Prior said that made her think that he supposed Richeldis killed Conrad?'

'She said Dan said "He should have died hereafter".'

'Sounds wrong,' he objected.

'It's a quote, you barmpot, don't you know anything?'

'Nope, I'm just a peasant. A bus driver from north of Watford.'

'It's *Macbeth*. I did it for GCSE.'

'We did the *Dream*. I don't think I ever finished it.'

'Well, Macbeth says it of Lady M after she kills herself.'

'Doesn't seem to fit.'

'No, well, if you reverse the sexes—'

'Hey up. Can't have any funny business.'

Rita indicated her disapproval of this by staring at him. Trevor tried another tack.

'So where's he buried then? Or did they cremate?'

'He wanted the parish church in the village. So that's where he is.'

'There'll have to be some sort of service for him, won't there? I mean you can't just bury him at dead of night and never a funeral note from the ramparts.'

'Mrs G, ahead of the game as usual, says they're going to have a memorial service for him Saturday week in the chapel here, though Richeldis wanted it in Oxford but Brink wouldn't let her. It was in *The Times* last week.'

'Wasn't in the *Sun*.' Trevor was so delighted with his scoring this one he guffawed outright. 'So who's going to be the new Warden?'

'I'm not too sure how they do these things. I suppose Matt Brink'll do the honours in the meantime.'

'Bit of a silly billy.'

'Right. At least Duff was impressive. Looked the part and that. All that white hair and white eyelashes and pale pinko-eyes. I've never known anyone with white eyelashes.'

'Put the fear of God into me,' he agreed.

Matthew Brink, from the late Conrad Duff's study in Bishop's House, heard the voices of students returning to college for the new term as the morning wore on. There would be a full house by supper time. Cars, motorbikes and the odd taxi crunched across the gravel; voices, mostly male with a wide variety of accents, moved past his room on the way to the bursar's office. It was like a dry pool slowly flooding from some hidden source after drought. He thought of the life flowing back into the place and then of the life that had left it so unexpectedly a month ago. Resentment swept over him. He should have died hereafter. No, that was wrong. *She* should have died. Well, it would have been better if Richeldis had died. She'd been a drain on Conrad for years, in his view. *He* might not have been so difficult if *she* hadn't been so perverse, she and her idiot son both.

What would that woman do with Conrad's suicide note? And where was it now? Say she produced it to the trustees when they descended. It would damage the Church, it would damage the college. His own career might well come to an end. He felt resentment that it had to be Conrad who died while Richeldis lived on. He felt aggrieved, as he looked round the chaotic room, that he would have to cope with the remains of Conrad's academic life.

He'd made a start on the first of two immense filing cabinets in Conrad's study. The room, originally the principal drawing room of the house, was across the hall from his own smaller one. *Its* ceiling did not leak. After half an hour he had realised that there was no order in the filing compartments. Duff had simply stuffed papers in as he wished to get rid of them. If there was any order, it was roughly chronological since, as one drawer filled up, Duff had been forced to move on to another. Brink had therefore begun to sort the papers by subject. He'd started at nine o'clock putting related files of material on the desk. By ten he had had to move on to the table under the window. Eleven had seen him at the sofa and now, as it neared noon, he was placing files like rows of seedlings on the uncarpeted floor. He felt it was an indignity, one of the many, which Duff had inflicted on him.

But he remembered, too, his earlier acquaintance with Conrad. He remembered when he'd first seen him in Christ Church chapter house, at 5 p.m. on the first Friday of his first Michaelmas term. E. R. Dodds had been lecturing on Plotinus to an audience of five undergraduates by the light of a single reading lamp. He hadn't understood a single word. But he'd gone on attending for the full eight weeks. It had formed his view of what scholarship was. The antiquity and beauty of the setting, the incomprehensibility of what he was sure were profound truths had brought him back week by week; that, and the pleasure of gazing at Conrad Duff's striking profile as it caught the light from the reading lamp on Dodds's desk.

Had he become a priest because he thought that scholarship was the same as holiness? If so, had he mistaken the basis of faith? He had long ago abandoned any pretension that he could follow in such footsteps. Over the last few years he'd given up reading works of scholarship entirely. Instead he read the reviews and told anecdotes about the foibles of scholars he had known or at any rate observed in the past. Or had he become a priest because Conrad Duff had taken orders? He had not gained Duff's friendship at Oxford. He'd not had the courage to do more than swim about in the outer circle. Later he'd met the more accessible Wade who had filled his need to worship.

But if scholarship had receded and friendship failed as an inspiration, there was still the institution of the Church, Brink felt. That at least must be an ark which endured. How would the trustees appoint a new Warden? Would they advertise and go through all that stupid palaver of job descriptions and interviews in the modern manner, or would they adhere to the traditional methods, tap into the old boy network and slide in someone who'd caught their random eye or to whom the Bishop owed a favour? Getting the right person into the right post was so very important if the Church were to flourish, to regain lost ground. He counted the ground the Church of England had lost recently: financially, and at Lincoln and in Sheffield in moral authority. To Brink in the 1960s the Church of England had seemed like a good bet. It had offered an assured social position and scope for doing good without too much discomfort. He had felt in his more exhilarated moments that Christians were the leven in the lump of the world; that places like Gracemount were settings in which Paradise could be created without the serpent. He would do his very best to see that it continued.

Almost involuntarily, Matthew began to mutter the *Nunc Dimittis*. 'Now lettest thou thy servant depart in peace according to thy word.' But he didn't want to die, did he? And anyway his eyes had not seen salvation. Salvation as an end had escaped him. It had grown fainter with the passing years. Something had gone wrong with his life plan. And that going wrong had somehow been linked to Conrad Duff. Somehow it was all Conrad's fault.

When Conrad had entered his life again, when, that is, he'd got his lectureship at Gracemount, it had taken him some time to make up his mind about the older, more mature Conrad. He had, when Matthew came into post, a tremendous reputation. A brilliant man, scholar and spiritual leader, just what the Church needed, some said. Others said he was a viperous, manipulative egoist, just what the Church didn't need. But Matthew had been prepared to be entranced. He could not shake himself free from that first romantic image of the youthful Conrad at Oxford twenty years before.

Working with Conrad as a colleague had seemed to offer a resurrection, a second chance at living properly. But it hadn't turned out like that. He remembered the times when Conrad had humiliated him, making him seem naive and clumsy. Conversation with him had been like a wrestling match with a well-greased opponent who knew a lot more holds than he did. He couldn't talk to him or interact with him in any simple way. Every conversation was a competition, every exchange had to be managed. It had all been such a strain. Sometimes Matthew wondered if he had *imagined* his love for Conrad, whether the whole range of his feelings was just a chimaera. But Matthew had admired him all the same. Conrad had only to crook his finger, offer a kind word, and Matthew would come running. Conrad could be enormously convincing, especially when he spoke of his vision of the Church's place in society, its need, its right to lead. Such a vision had seemed to offer security and dignity to one of Matthew's temperament. It was just that as the years went by, it became impossible to close one's eyes to the fact that leadership for Conrad meant the furtherance of his own place in that political scene, the furtherance, to put it crudely, of Conrad's ambition.

It had come to seem to Matthew that Conrad never did anything which did not contribute to the advancement of his career. He entertained with intent. He published widely on social and political topics. The mundane duties of running the college had claimed less and less of his attention. What had he wanted? Head of an Oxbridge House, bishopric, seat in the Lords? Matthew wasn't sure. But what he had been sure about was that, just before he died, Conrad had taken some sort of step forward. Something had happened which contributed to his progress up the ladder. It was Richeldis who had warned him. 'Conrad's last act,' she'd said. 'He's been burning the midnight oil on it. It's going to knock 'em for six.' Richeldis used what she took to be the talk of chaps, only she used the lingo of her youth, the fifties. Matthew had been consumed by curiosity. So what was it Richeldis knew about? He'd watched and waited. Finally, he'd been rewarded. He'd glimpsed the papers on Conrad's desk and of course he knew what they meant. It had been a shock. He'd not known what to do. But then they had disappeared. When he'd first started to go through Conrad's stuff a day or two after his death he could find no trace of them. And now he simply must find them again. They must not get into anyone else's hands. Brink surveyed the littered desk, sofa and floor. Wherever they were, he must find them.

The solicitor's words came back to him. The man had telephoned him within a week of Duff's death. 'The deceased has named you as his literary executor in the expectation, as he put it, that you will manage to publish at least one volume of political essays from the material in manuscript.'

'Yes,' Matthew had replied, 'yes, I see. Well . . .' What he felt was hurt that Conrad had not entrusted the finishing of his great work *The Darkened Glass* to his hands. What did he want done with that?

'Any material relating to *The Darkened Glass*,' the lawyer had continued, 'should be destroyed according to my client's wishes. And there is a codicil, perhaps rather an odd one, of recent date, which you'll need to know about and adhere to.' The man sounded almost threatening. 'The deceased forbids you to publish or deal with work done between May and November 1996.' But then, Matthew reflected, Conrad hadn't lived as long as November. He'd been dead by early September.

A shout of laughter from the garden brought him back to the present. He'd have to take on Conrad's teaching in addition to his own; New Testament studies as well as nineteenth-century church history. He felt fresh resentment at the thought of the demands of a new term and new students. He could scarcely restrain audible groaning at the prospect of going over the same old watered-down bits of scholarship with pupils, most of whom lacked every sort of equipment, linguistic, historical or spiritual, for their interpretation. Even before Conrad's death he had come to doubt the effectiveness of this way of training priests. It was a strain, too, having to be so everlastingly enthusiastic. But then the clergy had to give a lead, didn't they? That was what they were for, as Conrad had always said.

Brink thought of the last time he'd seen him, the day he'd died. He'd thought at first after they had carried him in that he would open his eyes and laugh at them for being mistaken. But when Conrad had at last opened his eyes he'd not laughed. Brink had seen vacancy in them and then terror, and then the sweat had begun to pour off him.

Brink had been present at the beginning of the end. Some parts of those three hours were still vivid in his memory, others he preferred to forget. It had been a perfect September day. The two apple trees outside the Warden's study window had begun to smell of their ripening fruit. Conrad had been sitting writing under the shade of one of them. A small table at his side held his books. He affected a wide-brimmed grey hat which had the look of a nineteenth-century American estate owner. When the moment of Conrad's collapse had come, Brink could remember only the panic he'd felt and then the resolution. He remembered carrying him upstairs to his bedroom with Aidan Prior. How heavy he'd been for so slight a man! His feet had bumped sickeningly on the stairs as they had tugged and heaved him a step at a time. He remembered hearing Richeldis's footsteps crunching the gravel and her voice hoarse at having to rise above her normal low tones. At first he'd resented young Prior being there but then perhaps it had been providential. Prior had insisted they sent for a doctor and together they had waited, not knowing whether they were intruding or offering support. In the end he'd sent Prior off to get the reserved sacrament from the chapel. When Richeldis and Crispin at last returned the two of them had stood at the foot of the bed staring down at Conrad rigid on the heaped pillows. He had felt the collusion between mother and son, united against a father neither of them had esteemed.

Brink closed his eyes to put the vision of the stuffy room from him. He looked up as the chimes of the chapel clock struck twelve. His eye caught the sepia print of Thomas Henry Newcome on the wall above the filing cabinet. Broad forehead, honest, manly gaze and full growth of beard and whiskers looked down on him. What did he know about it? It was all right for him, replete with moral and spiritual integrity. The rest of us don't have it quite so easy.

Theodora fingered the thick cream writing paper with its embossed address, Saplings, The Lane, Gracemount, and looked again at the fine flowing signature, Maria Locke Tremble.

She remembered Mrs Locke Tremble. She'd been a friend of her father's, a visitor to the north Oxford vicarage when Theodora was home from school. As a child she had been fascinated by Mrs Locke Tremble's steel-framed glasses, with lenses so thick they obscured

her eyes and meant one had to guess her meaning
from the tone of her voice. Since she was French by
birth and retained a slight accent including the French
'r', that wasn't always possible. Moreover, Mrs LT was
a musicologist (Dr LT had been a cathedral organist)
and Theodora knew nothing of that recondite trade;
thus her father's acquaintance had been something
of an enigma.

Theodora tapped the letter in her hand. How on earth
had the woman known she was here? And what did
she mean when she wrote, 'I have great need of you,
as you may have of me.' Was she one of those tedious
souls who hope to make themselves interesting by
suggesting a mystery where none exists? Theodora
surveyed the morning's notes spread out on the table
of her attic room. She'd avoided the refectory so as not
to have to talk to anyone and break the train of thought.
The remains of a college sandwich, cut to assuage the
appetite of the growing male young who would be on
the rugger pitch this afternoon, lay to one side.

She had had a productive morning marshalling
material in the library. The librarian hadn't appeared
but the cataloguing had presented no more eccen-
tricities than most theological libraries. Theodora, an
old hand, soon cracked the code and had it working
for her. Newcome's diaries for 1877 to 1878 lay in their
shiny black covers waiting for her attention. She had
not been able to trace the ones for '78 to '79 which
would be crucial but there was time enough to track
them down. As she began reading, she realised how
much she knew about Newcome's thought and how
little about his domestic tastes or indeed his comings
and goings. Her first task was chronology. Then, too,

it was obvious she would have to do some work on his wife to whose unstinting support the dedication paid tribute. There were a couple of her diaries and a box file of her letters which she intended to look at after supper. In a word, there was much she wanted to press on with. Gazing at the mound of material, she didn't know when she had been so happy. She did not wish to be interrupted.

Mrs Locke Tremble's note, pushed under her door to await her return, was, therefore, an intrusion. She didn't want to have to think about her. She looked at it again.

Dear Theodora (if I may),
When your father died so unexpectedly, I did not write to express the condolences which I keenly felt. I wonder if you would allow me to repair that omission now?

As you see, I have retired to the rustic life – always so wholesome, in the shadow of your pious institution. I would so very much value a reclaiming of your acquaintance [That would probably go better in French, Theodora felt]. Moreover, I have great need of you, as you may have of me. Will you do me the honour of taking five o'clock tea with me this afternoon? I do hope so.

Yours truly,
Maria Locke Tremble

There was a postcode but no telephone number, so if she wanted to reply she'd have to go in person. Theodora havered. Self-interest was beginning to win when there was a brisk knock at the door.

'Mr Ngaio, how very nice.'

'I hope you are well?'

'I am very well. Are you well?'

'Indeed, I am well.'

'And you have lunched, I hope?'

'I have had the pleasure of lunching with my sponsor, Mr Trevor Fisher. It is on Mr Fisher's behalf that I have taken the liberty of calling on you.'

'Ah.' Theodora waited.

'We wondered if you would do us the honour of taking coffee with us. I am by way of being your neighbour in this building.'

Hell's teeth, Theodora thought. Gracemount was much too sociable. She'd already had an invitation to Brink's beginning of term party on Monday evening, and now this. Which is more important, writing the definitive biography of one of the leading figures in the catholic revival such that it could inspire a new generation of catholics in the Church of England, or cementing relations with members of the Anglican communion from the developing world and an assortment of the aspiring youth?

'That is most kind of you, Isaiah. I'd love to join you.'

Isaiah's grave smile rewarded her.

Rita Nougatt said, 'Pleased to meet you,' and Trevor said, 'Hi, there.'

Rita stirred powdered coffee into mugs and topped it off with powdered milk. Trevor poured water from the kettle. Theodora remembered that this was how students lived and thought how little she wanted to do this, how there wasn't any aspect of the domestic life of students with which she was not totally familiar and how utterly reluctant she was to renew acquaintance with it. Nothing, she feared, was going to be said or thought over the next half hour which would be of the least interest. She resigned herself to being agreeable. The room was welcomingly warm because there was a fire burning in the grate. Theodora thought this was enterprising and said so.

'Isaiah's working his way round the logs at the back of the gatehouse,' Trevor said as though producing a particularly talented pupil.

'My problem is kindling. The small sticks are all too wet in your autumn weather. Neither, I think, shall I have much time to gather them. At home, of course, that task belongs to the women.'

Trevor was delighted. 'There you are, Rita. That's your vocation.'

Rita said, 'It's a perfectly honourable thing to do in itself. It's just that the chaps don't acknowledge that it is.' She turned to Theodora. 'Stephany says you've decided not to be priested.'

Theodora nodded.

'Why is that?' Rita pursued in her direct, social services way.

Theodora thought, it serves me right for prejudging people. 'Well, there's the thing about can we go it alone and still claim to be part of the universal catholic Church,' she replied.

'That all?' Trevor asked innocently.

Theodora stopped herself from saying that that was quite enough. Rita forestalled her. 'Trevor doesn't know much history so it doesn't weigh too much with him.' Her tone, though, was protective.

Isaiah Ngaio, who did know some church history (had he not carefully learned it?), nodded his approval.

'I'm going down that road myself,' Rita went on. 'But what I reckon is that if we, I mean women, really mean we want to change the structures, kick out all the stagging and grabbing and bullying that the chaps rely on,' she glanced affectionately at the unthreatening Trevor, his home-knitted pulley plucked and bulging like a lawn struck by moles, 'if we're really going to change those, we can't also grab bits of power within those structures.'

'Steph Prior doesn't agree with you,' said Trevor, quite happy to stir it. 'She reckons you've got to get in there where the action is. Sitting behind the tea urns is useless, she says.'

Isaiah wasn't sure he followed but he certainly approved of this woman's decision to take a back seat. He looked at Theodora, a different kettle of fish, if he mistook him not.

'It's difficult, isn't it, though?' Theodora knew her way round these arguments like the controls of a familiar car. 'I agree we need to have totally different structures and we ought to be imagining what these might be. While we're still enmeshed in the traditional ones, all of them orientated, as you say, towards worldly power, it's impossible to generate change. One of the reasons why I'm trying to get this life of Newcome finished is because he does seem to me to have an extraordinary insight into the effects of rigid social systems on the lives of ordinary Christians. If we can know what has been, is being done to us, perhaps we can find some alternatives which are theologically reputable.'

'I have great faith,' said Trevor, 'in the parish system.'

'Right,' Rita patted him. 'Nothing wrong with the parishes, pet. It's the big systems, national and international, which are so attractive to you lads so you get led astray.'

'My country would indeed be a benighted one if your great-grandfathers had not thought about international mission,' said Isaiah.

'Oh, mission's different.' Rita put him straight. 'I'm talking about ruling people. And what parishes should do is train people how to pray not how to vote. That's what priests are primarily for. The rest is flummery.' She'd worked out her position.

'So we need bishops elected by parishes, on five-year contracts only, nonrenewable.' Rita and Trevor got under way, their litany clearly familiar and well-honed.

'No seats in the Lords.'

'Abolish Synod.'

'Depoliticise.'

'No archbishops necessary.'

'Abolish archdeacons.'

'Downsize rural deans.'

'What about cathedrals?'

'Only monks and nuns need apply.'

'To the barricades, citizens.'

'So what are we doing here?' Theodora asked quietly.

'Church history, church liturgy, church doctrine, New Testament studies, Old Testament studies,' Trevor intoned.

'Can't pray, that lot,' Rita concluded.

'There's always Stephany keeping us alert to our context, bless her,' Trevor consoled her.

'But under the rule of Conrad Duff who only cared about on and up. Bound to the past, the old power structures . . .' Rita left the consequence open.

'But Richeldis had him by the heels,' Trevor said, as though this settled matters.

The village of Gracemount had ancient buildings but modern habits. The houses were too sensitively painted; their gardens were too trim; the village shop was a delicatessen. Only on the edge of the village where farmhouses without gardens hugged the road but looked backwards over their shoulders towards the acres which stretched up as far as the hills, only there was there a feeling of lived lives rooted in real work and sustained by neighbours. For the rest, it was too easy to commute to London or Oxford for a society to have established itself.

The man next door to the Saplings, at the Firs, was cutting his hedge and shouting at it as he did so. 'Get down, blast you, get in there,' he shouted as he snipped away, furiously wielding his shears. He was balanced on a stool so that he towered over his privet as though to subdue it. Theodora thought she had never seen such emotional energy put into hedge cutting. He looked up as she passed, meeting her eyes and looking through her as though she were an aspect of the weather.

The Saplings was a solid red brick villa with mock Tudor beams. The front garden, no more than three metres from gate to front door, was laid out with miniature box hedges interspersed with fine gravel. Standing to attention on either side of the black painted front door were two bay trees in terracotta pots.

Theodora wondered how far the French influence extended. The doorbell produced a crescendo of high-pitched squeals easily recognisable as a pug having hysteria. Will it be called 'Fifi'? Theodora wondered.

Mrs Locke Tremble had scarcely changed at all in the fifteen years since Theodora had last seen her. The figure, always slight, had shrunk and bent a little, the tremendous glasses still furnished the face and obscured the eyes. The wiry ginger hair stood out like a ruff round the thin, pale face.

Theodora was embraced on both cheeks. But the drawing room was actually rather English, full of chintz and horse brasses. On the oak table were piles of sheet music. In the gloom at the back of the room was what Theodora identified after a moment as a chamber organ. At either end of the mantelpiece stood two oval silver-framed photographs in black and white. The right-hand one showed a middle-aged man in pince-nez, perhaps Dr Locke Tremble, seated at an organ keyboard. The other one, also of a man, seemed familiar. After a moment Theodora realised she was looking into the eyes of her father aged about twenty-five and dressed for cricket.

Mrs Locke Tremble followed Theodora's gaze. 'Your dear father. A man of great *esprit*.'

'Yes,' said Theodora, 'he was.'

'And you resemble him?'

'Only in height.'

'But you serve the Church, yes?'

'I'm in deacon's orders.'

'And you have a connection with the institution on the hill?'

It took Theodora a moment to realise she referred

to Gracemount. 'I'm researching a life of its founder, Thomas Henry Newcome. They have the archive of his private papers, so I'm spending a week getting to grips.'

'That is excellent,' said her hostess as though Theodora had ratified an already known agenda. 'We will take a cup of tea and I will then reveal the reason for my mysterious summons. Fifi, leave our guest alone.'

The pug spared her mistress not a glance but continued to snuffle through her truncated nose at Theodora's shoes and skirt. Carefully Theodora advanced a hand towards her and after a moment the little bitch decided that all was well and rolled away towards the kitchen, the creamy fur wrinkled in tight folds round her shoulders like an ill-fitting pullover. I bet there'll be a spirit kettle, thought Theodora.

'China or Indian?' Mrs Locke Tremble called from the recesses of her kitchen.

'China would be agreeable, if you have it.'

Mrs Locke Tremble emerged with an enormous silver tray laden with a silver tea service and a plate of tiny cucumber sandwiches. Dexterously she lit the spirit kettle and set the immense teapot upon it. Ought to be either Fuller's walnut cake or madeleines, Theodora guessed. Mrs Locke Tremble darted back into the kitchen. There was the sound of tins being opened and she re-emerged with a good-looking walnut cake and a plate of small, dry madeleines. Theodora's lunch had been Spartan. She was delighted to see it all. As the tea filled the china cups she was aware of a ritual supported by history and literature. She rose to the occasion.

'Have you been here long, Mrs Locke Tremble?'

'Maria. Please. Gerald,' she nodded towards the photograph on the mantelpiece, 'died a year before your good father, though with more reason since he was a third older than Nicholas,' replied Mrs Locke Tremble mathematically. 'In the way of the unworldly he had forgotten to arrange about a pension. The Church which he served for thirty-seven years was not disposed to do anything for his widow, so I sold everything except his little organ, seized the copyright of his original pieces and retired, as you see, to rusticate.' She gestured with her hand at the solid comfort of the mock Tudor. 'I was fortunate to have my skill.'

Theodora understood her to mean her musicological knowledge.

'I was saved from total penury by the revival of interest in early music. It has most fortuitously demanded of me a great deal of work.' Mrs Locke Tremble was complacent. Theodora was glad that someone was benefiting from the modern delight in untunable sackbuts and ten-foot stopless horns.

'You will perhaps know,' Mrs Locke Tremble's tone merely hinted that she had turned to the business part of the meeting, 'that the Warden of the institution on the hill has recently passed away.'

Theodora nodded.

'You have perhaps met his wife, his widow?'

Theodora shook her head.

Mrs Locke Tremble sighed. 'She is indeed a woman of sorrows.' She leaned forward. 'He was not a good man.'

Theodora was not too sure how to take this. Looking

concernedly interested was a safe bet.

'Ah, but yes. He was not sympathetic to her, to his poor wife.'

Theodora considered this. Much depended what was meant by 'sympathetic'.

'But yes. It is well known. Though that is not the matter on which I wish to engage your help. Richeldis, the wife, is a dear friend of mine. It is on behalf of her son that I consult you. You have met Crispin?'

'I think so.'

'Yes, well, there is but one child. Her difficulty is that the boy blames himself for the death of his father.'

'I think I gathered that.'

'What she desires is that whoever killed her husband should be identified. And she has chosen you to undertake that great risk.'

For once Theodora was stumped. Who was barking mad here? Richeldis, Crispin or Mrs Locke Tremble? 'What?' was the most she managed.

'She does not want her dear Crispin to go forward into the world with that burden of guilt upon his young shoulders.'

'But . . .' Theodora did not know where to begin.

'You are right to ask, why not the police? But you will appreciate that there are some matters so delicate that the crude methods of the professionals are absolutely forbidden.'

'Well, er . . .'

'You see, whoever killed the Warden will certainly wish to keep the guilt focused upon the son who, as I say, already accuses himself.'

'But look here, how do you mean, "killed the Warden"? I understood that Conrad Duff died of a heart attack. Why should Richeldis or her son suppose otherwise?'

'The two of them, father and son, had a quarrel. The usual thing of young men and fathers. But it became heated. The young Crispin accused his father of several matters.'

'When did this happen?'

'The morning of the day he died.'

'Crispin feels he brought on the heart attack or whatever?'

'That is the young man's feeling.'

'Is it possible he is right?'

'No. No.'

'Because?'

'Because Richeldis knows for sure that between Crispin quarrelling with his father and Conrad having his attack there was another cause at work, far more shocking to Conrad, far more hurtful. It was that which for sure killed him.'

'Well, if she knows that, why doesn't she seek out that cause herself?'

'That is her problem. She does not know exactly who was the perpetrator and it is that which she wishes discovered. Also the exact form of the threat.'

'What threat?'

'The threat which killed Conrad.' Mrs Locke Tremble had all the triumph of one who completes a circular argument.

'But why me?'

'Because everyone else who might be asked to undertake the inquiry is a suspect.'

'Why doesn't she ask me herself?'

'I have the pleasure of being acquainted with you

and,' she gestured towards the photograph, 'your family.'

'Look, I really don't think . . .' Theodora was appalled.

'I said in my letter that we might be able to help each other. You spoke of your great work, your lifework, *n'est-ce pas*?'

Theodora retreated to nodding again.

'And for that purpose you need the whole archive of Thomas Henry Newcome, yes?'

'Yes.' Theodora wondered what on earth was coming next.

'Richeldis has part of that archive. A part which may be very important to your work. It is Newcome's letters and diaries of himself and of his wife for the year eighteen seventy-eight to nine. The time, the very year, I believe, immediately before his great published work *Cities of Men, City of God*.' Mrs Locke Tremble leaned forward in her chair and smiled up at Theodora. 'She will release those diaries to you on the completion of your task, when you can reveal the perpetrator of her husband's death.'

CHAPTER FOUR

High Table

The parish church of Gracemount lay at the end of
the village beyond the bridge which carried the road
uphill to the college. The living was in the gift of the
college. The college's council had not resisted the
temptation to put in men of sufficient academic weight
to help with its teaching load. Over the years of the
twentieth century the villagers had had to put up with
the ministry of an Aramaicist, a specialist in Byzantine
liturgies and the best known British authority on
Hittite magic texts. Sometimes the village felt its
pastoral needs were being neglected. Sometimes the
PCC, always two men and two women, none of whom
would see sixty again, longed for an ordinary Anglican
ignoramus in his thirties with a wife who would take
the Mothers' Union seriously and two point four
children and a dog. Their cries had gone unheeded
until the most recent incumbent. He at least was in
his thirties and married. He had no children but he
did have a dog. The Reverend Tobias Spin doubled as
the librarian at Gracemount St Sylvester and had the

task of supervising the preaching course for ordinands in their final year.

Toby Spin thought of himself as young. He wore a lot of denim and Doc Martens. His favourite words were 'relevant' and 'flexible'. He played the guitar well and the organ, which he referred to as 'keyboard', passably. He genuinely liked young people and they responded by liking him. 'He means well,' said his (older) colleagues, and he did. A lesser man, late on this rainy Saturday afternoon, would have tired as he put the fifth ordinand in succession through his preaching paces. But Toby put the same energy into the fifth as he had into the first candidate.

Theodora, seeking calm after the turbulence of her tea with Mrs Locke Tremble, had walked up to the parish church to give herself time to reflect on the extraordinary proposition put to her. She saw the light in the choir, paced between the yew trees and stepped down into the tiny nave.

'Bounce it off a corbel,' Toby called. He was stationed halfway down the nave with a stopwatch in his hand. At the nave steps, standing unlevelly, weight on one leg, Theodora could make out Trevor, a sheaf of paper clutched in his left hand.

'You're doing splendidly, really marvellous stuff, but you're inaudible beyond the second row.'

'What?' inquired Trevor.

'Throw your head back, breathe from your diaphragm and aim at the angels.'

'What? Where?'

Theodora glanced up at the angel faces smiling candidly down from between the nave pillars. The

building was Norman below but the fourteenth century
had renewed the roof vaulting with splendour.

'I don't seem to be able . . .' Trevor mumbled.

'Can't hear,' said Toby clearly.

'I said "the acoustics".'

'No bad acoustics, only bad preachers,' said Toby.

Theodora warmed to the man for having standards.

'What about a mike?' Trevor wheedled.

'If you can't fill a space this size without a mike
you might as well jack it in. Now, just once more. The
last bit. Something about love.'

'The Gospel teaches us,' Trevor mumbled, one eye
on the corbelled angel, 'that we need someone to love
just as much, perhaps a bit more, than we need
someone to love us.' Trevor reluctantly shared his
insight. 'We can't do that, I mean we can't either give
or receive love, not real love, unless we first fix our
hearts on God . . .'

'Right. Right. That's super. Let's leave it there for
now.'

Toby has a background in theatre production,
Theodora thought, unlike Trevor, who has a background in bus driving. Not for the first time Theodora
rejoiced in the capaciousness of the Church of England
which offered scope for so many talents, even if its
management of them faltered.

Theodora's first reaction when she grasped what
Mrs Locke Tremble was saying about the missing
sources for Newcome's life had been anger. Had she
laboured so long and sacrificed so much precious leisure
to be thwarted in this mad way? What were they all
playing at up at Gracemount? This demure French
widow was indulging in blackmail, though she saw it,

clearly, as nothing more than a sensible business transaction.

'I'll have to think about it.' Theodora had been austere.

'*D'accord*,' said her hostess. 'But not for too long. Time is of the essence. I believe Gracemount has, what did my dear husband call them, a visit, no, a visitation this week. I fear that if matters are not resolved to her satisfaction before that event occurs, Richeldis is minded to petition the visitors and spill the beans.' Mrs Locke Tremble relished her own grasp of idiom.

At first Theodora had thought she would seek out Aidan and share the story. He, after all, was her oldest friend in this community. But now that the opportunity offered, she might as well check one or two points with the librarian.

Toby was struggling into a Barbour, Trevor was zipping his anorak.

'Mr Spin?'

'Hi. It's Theo, isn't it? Thelma mentioned you'd want to have a word. Sorry I haven't got round. Beginning of term. Pretty hectic.' He waved his hand in Trevor's direction. 'Have you raided the archive yet?'

'I dipped into it this morning.'

'Got what you want? It's Newcome's letters and diaries, isn't it?'

'Yes. And I think there are some of his wife's papers as well. I've got his for pre eighteen seventy-eight but not hers, Esther's. And I haven't got either of them for seventy-nine.'

'Oh good. That's fine then.' Spin was dutifully enthusiastic.

'I was wondering about seventy-eight to seventy-nine. *Eighteen* seventy-nine,' Theodora repeated in case Spin had mistaken the century.

'You need that as well?' Spin's tone suggested she was exorbitant in her demands.

'He published *Cities of Men, City of God* at the end of that year.'

'Right.' Spin was reassuring. He knew which century was which.

'Do you know where the material for that year might be kept?'

'Kept? Me? Well, no. I'm not really that sort of librarian, if you see what I mean. All I do is collect the orders from the rest of the staff for the stuff they want put in, measure them against the derisory financial allowance the Warden agrees to for the library and pass the orders to Thelma for processing.'

Never make anyone feel guilty, was one of Theodora's pastoral maxims. But she was shocked all the same. How could a theological college, a centre of learning and training for the Church's most precious resource, not know what it possessed? She tried again.

'The material for seventy-eight to seventy-nine. It does figure in the catalogue.'

'Jolly good.'

'But it's not shelved with the other material for seventy-eight.'

'Had a good look round, have you?'

'I wouldn't say I was exhaustive.'

'Well then.'

'But why wouldn't it be shelved with the other material? I noticed there was space on the shelves.'

'Perhaps someone else has it out.'

'If so, they didn't sign it out, or anyway not recently. Who checks, by the way?'

'What?'

'Who checks the record, the signing in and out?'

'Well, I suppose if a lot of stuff went missing I'd notice. In time,' Spin admitted. 'And when there are essays due, the popular texts do disappear for a bit. But they pretty well always come back in the end.'

Theodora thought of all the well-run libraries she'd used in her time: Bodley, Ashmole, Doctor Williams, Senate House. 'Are there other spaces where bits of the Newcome archive might be lodged?'

Toby Spin shook his head in bewilderment. 'The bound stuff, as I understand it, is all in the library on the shelves. The loose leaf stuff is in his room.'

'His room?'

'In boxes.'

'Where's his room?'

'The Newcome room. It's in the turret above the Warden's room.'

'How can I get in?'

'Well, that's not too easy. You have to go through the Warden's apartment and then there's a staircase leading off the top floor.'

'Do I need a key?' Theodora was firm. Scholarship's demands could not be gainsaid.

'It's not so much a key. It's that you'd need to get past Richeldis.'

'Is Mrs Duff observing any sort of mourning for her husband?'

'Apart from dancing on his grave, I haven't seen any.' Toby had had enough of Theodora's importunity. Though a live and let live man, he didn't care for women who took themselves too seriously. He put Theodora into this category.

'Look, terribly sorry, but I must dash. Are you dining in hall?'

'Yes,' Theodora answered. 'Mr Brink has invited me. I look forward to meeting the rest of the staff.' Then she realised that with the Warden dead there were no more staff to meet. 'I mean the guests,' she said to Spin's retreating back.

Theodora watched him as he zigzagged round the graves in the direction of the vicarage. She regretted that she'd made him uneasy. Then she caught herself up. Toby Spin had a task, to be a librarian. He wasn't fulfilling it. He didn't know his stock or its value. He had no systems for checking its use. It was he or the institution that was at fault, not she. It was time she grew up and stopped blaming herself for other people's shortcomings.

She turned the opposite way to Toby. Though there was scarcely any daylight left now at seven o'clock, she wanted to locate the grave of her hero and his wife. Where would they be laid? The churchyard was humped with the layered dead of nine hundred years. Only the last two hundred years were marked by headstones. The graves on the south side were packed closely together. There was hardly space for the tussocky grass to push between them. But towards the north-east side, beside the holly hedge and shaded by a large beech, she came upon the purpose of her quest.

The Reverend Thomas Henry Newcome had chosen or had had chosen for him a plain square headstone in the enduring pink granite of Aberdeenshire. She could make out the inscription: 'In memory of Thomas Henry Newcome, priest, 1842 to 1899, who by his life and doctrine set forth God's true and lively word.'

It was the same epitaph as appeared on his memorial plaque in her own church of St Sylvester's Betterhouse. There were no signs of flowers or planting on the grave. The Newcomes had had only one child, a daughter, Christina, who had died in her eleventh year, of diphtheria. As far as Theodora's research could determine there were no direct descendants. Standing before the bleak grave, Theodora was swept by the commonplace melancholy of the surroundings. The hour, the place, were triste. Rooks cawed. A light wind stirred the beech leaves about her feet. It was a cliché of autumn and decay but no less potent for that. All human endeavour, however ardent, however spirited (and Newcome had been both in his life and work) came to this.

She turned from the husband to the wife. Rearing up half a dozen yards to her husband's left was a single mourning angel yearning over a slab tomb.

'In memory of Esther Bouverie Newcome née Chalfont, wife of the Reverend Thomas Henry Newcome. Born August 16th 1852, died February 12th 1889. "Leave me, O Love which reachest but to dust, and thou, my mind, aspire to higher things." '

How very odd, Theodora reflected, to find the lines of a seventeenth-century poet which might be thought more suitable for the husband than the wife. It was unusual, too, not to quote Scripture. Had Esther chosen her own memorial or had her husband, surviving her by a decade, done it for her? Perhaps when, if, she got her hands on the papers for the missing years, the point could be clarified. And that was the first matter in hand. To whom, in law, would the diaries belong? She understood that Newcome had left all his papers to the college which he had founded. Would that cut any ice with Richeldis?

Theodora began to make her way round the north side of the church. The path lay near the wall of the building. At the far side she could see the wicket gate which would take her to the track which ran uphill through the woods to Gracemount. But between the path and the gate was a figure. It was bent over a hump in the ground. Theodora recognised a newly covered grave which lacked a headstone. Standing looking down at the raked earth was a woman. In one hand she held a torch, in the other a packet of post-cards. She wore a dark cloth coat and a headscarf from which long strands of grey hair had escaped. Theodora made to pass her by but as she did so the woman turned and looked her full in the face. Then she looked down at the cards in her hand.

'I am trying out my husband's, my late husband's, epitaph.'

The voice was low, modulated, what Theodora thought of as a female don's voice. It had been the accompaniment of her childhood in her father's north Oxford vicarage.

'What do you think of "He died as he lived"? Or is that too cryptic?' The woman traced with her foot on the loose earth. It looked like the last letter of the Greek alphabet. 'Or how about "He aspired to alpha but ended in omega"? Or is that too much like a crossword clue?'

Before Theodora could reply, the woman flicked her wrist and the cards flew into a fan shape.

'Here,' she said. 'You choose. I have had such pleasure composing them. They are all apposite in their way. Every card an ace.'

Aidan Prior put the telephone down. There had been no answer. Through the open door of his study, on the floor of the living room, he could see his sons. Henry was carefully joining one piece of Meccano to another to construct one of those Pirenesi-like buildings which Stephany found so disturbing. Jamie, who was learning not to interfere with his brother's work, had evolved his own game round his activity. It consisted in crawling round in a circle crooning his latest new word, 'vroom'. Each was totally absorbed in his task. Was this the definition of innocence? Aidan wondered.

He could hear Stephany's step on the stairs. He felt he couldn't go on living like this: evading, prevaricating, constantly fending off the disabling past. He couldn't trust himself and so could trust no one else. He had thought for a time that Theodora's coming might be a help, but as soon as he had seen her at supper in his home he had realised there was no possibility of making her his confidante. It wasn't that she would judge him, it was the fact that she would not that he found intolerable. As for Stephany, whom he had loved for her crispness, what he called to himself her clean-shirtedness, she was just the person in his present pain that he could not turn to.

In half an hour he would have to dine in hall. It was unthinkable that on the first Saturday of term he should not. He would dine in the body of the hall with thirty other ordinands. Stephany would dine at high table with the other three, no, two staff. It would be the first hall without the Warden. Brink would surely have to make some sort of announcement. What would he say? 'Gentlemen and, er, Ladies, I regret to have to tell you that the Warden, the late Warden, took his own life four weeks ago. Fortunately, we think we can cover it up. Lists for church history tutorials are posted on the staff notice board. Please be sure to check your times. May I wish you all a very happy and blessed term.'

Well, no, probably not. He thought of Brink and the contempt he felt for him. He could not go on like this. He could not become a priest, that was clear. What was not clear was what else he could not do and what else he ought to do.

'Dan.' He heard Stephany's voice from the stairwell. 'Dan, sweetie, I've got to say a word to a couple of my keen first years before hall. Could you possibly give Henry and Jamie their supper? It's all ready. You just need to put a light under the soup for a minute or two.'

It was understood that Stephany's work took precedence over his. She, after all, was being paid.

'Sure.' He did not go to the door. He could not bear to see her. 'I'll do that.'

'Thanks, love. See you in hall.' She sounded anxious. He listened to her footsteps first hesitating then retreating down the stairs. Then he went back into the study and began to tap out his message on the old word processor. In the distance the bell for hall began to toll.

* * *

71

Unsure about how formal hall might be, and wishing to be on the safe side, Theodora had flailed her way into a black woollen dress which had belonged to an aunt even taller than she was. She was under the impression that this would allow her to be inconspicuous. In the distance she heard the refectory bell start to roll.

'You're much too smart,' said Stephany catching her up as she strode across the hundred yards between Newcome House and the refectory.

Theodora started, as though caught in some sort of backsliding. 'I had thought in terms of camouflage.'

'You thought wrong.'

Theodora scrutinised her friend. She wore a denim skirt and a very clean, crisp, starched pink cotton blouse which Theodora would not herself have chosen. She saw that Stephany sported a narrow clerical collar almost but not quite concealed by the collar of the blouse. Theodora wore a clerical collar in her pastoral work when visiting schools, hospitals and prisons. Otherwise she avoided it. She worked with a lot of priests to whom it would have given offence. Stephany presumably wore one for the same reason.

'They haven't thought up a proper evening dress for clerical women.'

'Nope,' Stephany agreed. 'All part of the current role and gender confusion endemic in our profession. The Warden, the late Warden, used to wear clerical evening dress. He'd have approved of you. Of course he was rehearsing for the time when he got the Presidency of Magdalen or whatever it was he wanted. And he liked dressing up.'

'What about the others?'

'Brink wears clerical black. Even Spin wears a jacket and tie, as do the students. Have you read Fleichman and Fleichman on dress codes in impermeable institutions?'

Theodora had to admit she'd missed that one.

'Affirmation of hierarchy, safety resulting from conformity.'

'No camouflage then?'

'Not to the trained eye,' Stephany said with satisfaction.

'In my youth,' Theodora said (she allowed herself the phrase), 'halfway through my second year, my college decided to admit men. Up to that time all the female high table used to change into evening dresses over or indeed under which for most of the year they wore cardigans. When the men came they left off the cardigans. I sometimes wondered why.'

'Stripping for action,' said the sociologist. 'Was that the only change?'

'No, just the most startling.'

The entrance hall into the refectory was small. There was a feeling of too many elbows, Theodora thought. Her height allowed her to review the troops.

'Matthew Brink,' said Stephany, fixing her eye on the tubby figure in clerical black. 'Theodora Braithwaite.'

'Miss Braithwaite, how very nice to make your acquaintance. I'm so sorry we haven't had a chance to meet before. I knew your remarkable father, of course.'

'Of course.'

'And may I introduce my guest for the evening, Dr Timothy Wade? A fellow historian, though not of your period. He's seventeenth century.'

Theodora looked down on a slim, delicate-featured man. His figure and movement were boyish, but his hair was strong, thick and grey, worn a shade longer than men of his generation had been brought up to. Very dark eyes did not smile back at her.

'I read your article on Newcome in last Michaelmas's JCH. You make him more interesting and more important than I'd thought him.'

Theodora reflected on the ambiguity of this. Was he praising the writing for identifying trends hitherto unsuspected by historians or was he sneering at her exaggeration of a minor figure to inflate the importance of her research? His tone was level and difficult to construe. Before she could respond, Brink had marshalled them into pairs and led them down the aisle between the refectory tables. He and Stephany led, then Theodora and Wade, then Mr and Mrs Spin. Bringing up the rear and alone, as though to symbolise the equivocal status of bursar, came Thelma Gainley.

The refectory's hum subsided as they filed in. Three tables of mostly men of mixed ages but mainly under forty turned towards the end where the shallow dais marked the difference between teachers and taught. The bell ceased to toll. They took their places. Then Brink stepped forward.

'Gentlemen and, er, Ladies, before we say grace, I would like you to join me in honouring the memory of our late Warden. Many of you will have heard of his untimely death. All of you will recall his tremendous efforts on your behalf as teacher, counsellor and friend. Some of you will have felt that he was a father to you.

We, his colleagues, are particularly aware of a gap in our common, collegiate, lives, which nothing can fill. Our sympathy, too, goes out at this time to his widow and son, to Richeldis and Crispin. We thank God for a life well lived to His glory. Shall we stand?'

It was all very decorous. But Theodora, watching the student body, thought she detected not sadness but relief, a definite lightening of the atmosphere. In the body of the hall she glimpsed Trevor sitting next to Isaiah Ngaio and opposite, flanked by the two other female ordinands, Rita. Theodora searched for, but could not find, Aidan.

'Toby says we're all going to get along just fine from now on,' Mrs Spin said, turning to Theodora for the soup. 'He's no loss, Toby says, and the liturgy will develop better without him. Conrad was more concerned about where you stand and what you wear than communication.' Mrs Spin put the sacred term in capitals. 'Of course I'm a Presbyterian myself so liturgy's not that important to me.'

Theodora took in the Northern Irish burr and the prominent thyroid eyes of Mrs Spin and thought how tiresome the next ten minutes were going to be.

'Of course, Toby's an authority on it. It's really his great thing and old Conrad wouldn't let him experiment at all. Toby says it's all out of date.'

Theodora glanced up the table and caught the voice of Mrs Spin's husband saying to Stephany, 'We've simply got to be flexible about this. The important thing is to develop something relevant to the man in the street. Lots of different approaches. Many mansions, type of thing. Jenkins is right really.'

Perhaps, Theodora thought, they only have one topic

between them or perhaps it's some sort of concerted campaign directed to changing prevailing college policy, embarked on with indecent haste.

'He wasn't a well man, Conrad Duff, you know. I was a nurse before Toby married me,' her accent deepened at the memory, 'and I could tell. And his wife,' Mrs Spin lowered her voice and bent intimately nearer Theodora's face, 'couldn't have cared less. She's cold, you know, very frosty.'

Since this seemed to be the common opinion of Richeldis, Theodora admired Mrs Spin's lowering of tone, presumably in respect for the dead.

'Do you know Mrs Duff well?'

'Oh, not hardly at all. She wouldn't look at the likes of me. Just a humble nurse, you see. Though I was good enough to get her the odd fix when she ran a wee bit short.'

'Fix?'

'In a manner of speaking. Things to keep you going. Like we all need from time to time.' Mrs Spin gazed into Theodora's eyes. 'Could you pass me the salt? The soup's a bit tasteless, don't you think?'

Theodora had scarcely noticed it. It was the familiar whitish brew, distantly related to chicken, with which she had started so many suppers in hall in the past.

'And you might pass me the mustard too. It'll cheer it up a bit.'

Theodora watched fascinated while Mrs Spin doctored the brew. This done, she drank it very rapidly.

'Have you lived in the village long?' Theodora pursued her social duty.

'We've been here four years. Toby served his title in Gainsborough. Then he went to Medwich for a year

as succentor. The close is very snooty there. Do you
know it at all?'

Theodora admitted she had a nodding acquaintance.

'Then he had a year in the chaplaincy at Bristol
University where he met me and we fell in love,' Mrs
Spin concluded simply as though Providence had
arranged all for just this end. 'I'd qualified in the
August at Bristol General and we got married in the
September. Have you a fiancé yourself, Miss
Braithwaite? Theodora, may I call you Theo?'

Theodora felt all that well-bred English women do
feel when assaulted by Celtic warmth and woman-
liness.

'Not right this minute.'

'It'll surely not be long, and you a handsome woman.
And some men like a tall girl.'

Theodora thought, I've been elaborately educated,
a great deal has been spent on me. I'm not without a
variety of worldly experience. Why have I not learnt
to cope with this sort of intrusiveness without snub-
bing? She took refuge in the historical perspective.
How odd that at this point in history Mrs Spin should
still suppose there was only one proper way of life for
a woman: marriage. Her thoughts went back to the
epitaph she had seen earlier this evening on the grave
of Esther Newcome. 'Leave me, O Love which reachest
but to dust.' She was saved, however, from having to
respond, for the soup plates were removed, the meat
appeared and she was free to turn to her other neighbour.

'Some of my students confuse T. H. Newcome with
Cardinal Newman.' Again there was the same level,
uninflected tone from Wade.

Theodora was delighted to be on her own ground. 'Yes, though of course Newcome was a very different fish. He seems never to have dallied with Rome. His Anglicanism was unshakable.'

'Like your own?'

'My family's been in it a long time.'

'But the current time is not the best?' Wade hazarded.

'We've seen worse. I wouldn't care to have lived under Cromwell.'

'A genuinely religious man,' said Wade, defending his own period.

'But not pleasant.'

'His enemies were not pleasant.'

'Pleasantness returned with Pepys,' Theodora suggested.

'An absolute charmer,' Wade agreed.

'I realise from my visit to the Newcome graves this evening that she, Mrs Newcome, Esther, must have overlapped with George Eliot in her prime.'

'It's odd to think they inhabited the same country let alone the same century, those two. I mean the Cardinal and George Eliot. Did they ever meet, do you know?'

'I don't think so. It would make one of those unimaginable conversations Van Loon specialised in. The one thing the Cardinal was not was an intellectual. Whereas she . . .'

'Provides the paradigm for one. Yes.'

'But they both have something in common,' Theodora went on.

'Namely?'

'Work, the idea that practice is what counts. The

Cardinal thinks of the spiritual life as work, Eliot of the moral life in the same terms. They are both far removed from our present-day delight in theory which is quite a different thing.'

'You think we've lost the habit?' Wade glanced round the hall.

'A lot of clergy seem to feel the Office is too much trouble.'

'Talk *about* prayer rather than actually praying.'

'Ordination courses seem to foster that spirit.' Theodora was regretful.

'Work is the salvation,' Wade agreed. 'And your man felt that too. After all, he left his monument.' Wade nodded at the portrait about the servery. 'All this we owe to Newcome.'

'Will it survive?' Theodora asked.

Wade hesitated before responding. 'If Duff had lived, yes, probably.'

'Because?'

'Simply because Conrad didn't like to be associated with failure and made certain what he took on succeeded.' Wade seemed to think he might have said too much. He made a great play of getting more potatoes to Theodora, then went on. 'What made you turn to biography as a vehicle for understanding history?'

Theodora considered this. 'I suppose I see human agency as the most important sort of causality. Also I like the detection element.'

'The slow revelation of bits of knowledge.'

'Exactly. And the pleasure of creating a picture step by step. Like portrait painting.'

'How do you know if you've got the right bits?'

'Criteria like consistency come in.'

'That's nothing more than plausibility under another name. Take your man, Newcome. What if you discovered something about him that you hadn't looked for, incest, say, or theft?'

'I simply shouldn't believe it. Anyway, with worthy subjects, biography is more than gossip. Great men are influenced by great ideals.'

Wade seemed to think he'd won his point. 'My grandfather, who died in nineteen sixty aged ninety-five, once met Newcome.'

'Did he leave an account?' Theodora turned professional.

'Only with me.'

'Pity. Hearsay is so difficult to use. Where did they meet?'

'Here. Newcome was no longer Warden but he lived on in the wing Richeldis and Conrad had. There's a room in the tower above the flat.'

Theodora nodded. 'What did they talk about?'

'My grandfather wanted to talk about *Cities of Men, City of God*, naturally.'

'But Newcome?'

'Was reluctant, apparently. Like trying to crank a car, said Grandad, who had experience of the ones you had to turn over with a handle. Newcome seemed to think the success of the book had been undeserved.'

'That it wasn't.'

'You rate it highly?'

'Yes. Don't you?'

'It's too earnest for me. A touch of the *Westminster Review* about it.'

'But the vision is remarkable.'

'But unrealised.'

'A measure of its quality.'

'I see you're a true believer.' Wade did not smile.

'I think it prompted my vocation.'

'How?'

'As you say, *Cities of Men* sees vocation as recognising that there are things that need to be done. Work at hand.'

'Not, then, in terms of an overwhelming inner conviction of one's specialness, some deep feeling.'

'Feeling is a bad guide.'

Tim Wade gazed at the remains of his chicken. 'I find your austerity daunting,' he said with finality. 'Perhaps you'd better return to Mrs Spin and her domesticities for the pudding. Which, if I'm not mistaken, will be bread and butter, this being the first hall of term.'

But Theodora was spared a second bout with Mrs Spin. In the body of the refectory there was a disturbance. Someone had come in late or uninvited. At the far end of the long room a thin, boyish figure in a blue tracksuit was being helped – or was it restrained? – by some of the students. The figure burst from their hands and sprang on to one of the tables. For a moment it seemed as though he rose from amid a sea of stretching hands as in some outlandish ballet.

'I want you to know, I want you all to hear . . .'

There were murmurs of 'Come on, old son. Take it easy.'

'I want you all to know,' the voice persisted, 'I killed my father.'

Theodora recognised Crispin Duff. It was Brink and Mrs Gainley who rose together and made their way rapidly down the hall.

* * *

A couple of hours later Theodora recalled the scene. As she put aside her notes in their orderly sequence she remembered how purposeful Thelma Gainley and Brink had seemed. Brink, who had looked so bumbling before supper, had proved quite incisive. They had led, indeed practically frogmarched, Crispin Duff out. Where had they stowed him? she wondered. With his mother back at the Warden's flat? Surely the young man was in need of help. But then, Theodora reflected, she had herself been invited, no, coerced into providing just that help by Mrs Locke Tremble's request. If Crispin was obsessed with guilt for his father's death, and if that guilt was unfounded, should she not help to free him from it by finding out what had happened?

She recognised how much she resented having to put aside her concern for the past, her precious research, and attend to the problems of the present moment. She resented even more the fact that her access to the past was controlled by how well she managed the present. Wade had asked her how she would know whether she'd got the truth about Newcome. She had said consistency. But she ought to have said evidence, the quality of it, its provenance and range. Now it seemed as though her ability to get the evidence about Newcome's last year before the publication of his book depended on her being able to get to the evidence for the events concerning the last hours of Conrad Duff's life. If Mrs Duff did possess the record for Newcome and his wife's life in that crucial period immediately before publication of *Cities of Men*, and if her price for making that information available was clearing her son of his delusions by finding out the truth, then there was no help for it, she would have to negotiate with the peculiar widow. Even if it was the Sabbath tomorrow, Theodora told herself, she would have to steel herself and seek out Richeldis.

CHAPTER FIVE

Research

Isaiah Ngaio closed his office book and drew the blanket from his bed round his shoulders. There was a chill beneath the mildness of the autumn morning, warning that the cold was the real weather, the warmth merely a legacy from the summer past. He had opened his window to make his orisons. At home, of course, he had said his first prayers of the day in the open air. Here he had hesitated. He had not seen anyone venture forth, as would surely have been most natural, to pace round the square lawn between Newcome House and the refectory and chapel block, book in hand, eyes concentrated. So presumably that was not how they did things here. The chapel clock struck the quarter. Forty-five minutes to go before the eight o'clock Communion. He would go forth and savour God's good gifts on this his first Sabbath in England. With reluctance he discarded the blanket, folded a plastic bag (given him by Rita) into the front of his makshi, and, thus equipped for whatever kindling he should chance upon, moved with sure step and dignified carriage downstairs.

The opening from the main drive to the ride, though not easily seen by someone who did not know of its existence, revealed itself to Isaiah. A hidden way and a difficult path was a path to salvation. Isaiah's was a mind formed on portent and omen, which are not far from metaphor. What he read in Scripture he found in life. No part of landscape was unsuffused by divine being or divine meaning. All configuration of wood and stone, all human presence and gesture had significance. As the Psalmist sang, so Isaiah thought and felt. Hence when he reached the pool and saw Crispin Duff kneeling in the thick bracken to its north singing to himself, he was not as taken aback as his English friends might have been. His hesitation about going forward was due not to surprise or embarrassment so much as to the wish of one religious man not to intrude upon another's devotions.

It was only gradually that Isaiah perceived that prayer was not what occupied Crispin. The youth was indeed kneeling, or at least sitting back on his heels. But attached to his ears were wires and at his side was what Isaiah recognised as a Walkman. These objects were not common in his home territory but sometimes they would appear clamped to the ears of a youth who had spent time in the city and come upon them as tokens of conspicuous prosperity or Western modernity. Isaiah regarded them with distaste. Such contraptions seemed to him to indicate dependence on the artificial and ephemeral. It was, he felt, a sort of idolatry.

Crispin turned a blank eye towards him. Then fretfully, as though freeing himself from fetters, he tore the earphones off. 'Have you ever killed anyone?'

Isaiah reflected. 'Only in my heart.'

'I've done that too.'

'Repentance will always call forth forgiveness.'

'But I can't stop hating.'

'Whom do you hate?'

'Myself, my father.'

'Count your blessings and act out of them.'

'What blessings would those be then?'

Isaiah looked down at this flimsy youth and thought of his own country. 'You ate well last night. You can read and write. You can journey from one end of this country to the other without men with Kalashnikovs demanding your deference. You have no right to your discontent, no right to your hatred. Your only proper emotion is gratitude.'

'You don't understand me.'

'There is One who does. Seek His path and healing will surely follow.'

But Crispin had been raised by and among people who considered the development of the self in all its florescent glory was the true end of man. His father had taught him life was a matter of imposing yourself on others; his mother that it was a matter of claiming your territory and defending it. 'Of course,' he said, choosing his weapon, 'it's all quite different for us.'

Isaiah felt he had said all that could be said. It was not, for him, a matter of argument. He gazed at Crispin for a moment longer and then strode off down the path towards the chapel.

The door to the Warden's apartment led off the entrance hall of Bishop's House. The hall was deserted.

No sound came from within the apartment or from the House itself. There was no answer to the bell. There was no answer to Theodora's knock. Mrs Duff had not appeared at the college Communion a couple of hours ago. Earlier, Theodora had obtained Mrs Duff's telephone number and rung. There had been no reply. Theodora considered writing a note, always her preferred method of communication with strangers, but Mrs Locke Tremble had insisted that time was of the essence. And so it was for Theodora too. She had but a week's precious leave. If she did not push her research forward during this time, Heaven knew when she might again be granted such an opportunity. Importunity was not in Theodora's nature. In her pastoral work, if people were unwilling to take what she could offer, she would not press. But here with her deepest interests at stake she could not be defeated.

She returned the way she had come and walked out on to the gravel in front of the entrance porch. Then she began to make her way round the building. The peeling sign on the wicket gate set in the tall yew hedge said 'Private. Warden's Garden'. Without hesitation Theodora strode through the narrow opening, brushing aside unlopped strands of old man's beard. A strip of roughly cut lawn shaded by apple trees opened before her. The fruit lay embedded and worm-eaten in the uneven grass. Hard against the house Michaelmas daisies faded and drooped, waiting for the first frosts to finish them off. In the corner by the French window was a stack of deck chairs, their bright canvas washed to a blur of stripes.

'We live in a decaying house, set in a decaying

garden, preparing young men to serve a decaying institution,' said a voice behind her.

Theodora swung round. Richeldis Duff stood a few yards away from her. She was dressed in a dark blue cotton smock which hung to below her calf; round her head was the scarf which Theodora had seen at the graveside. The effect was halfway between nun and peasant. Beside her was a basket filled with the equivocal fruit.

'Decay has its own beauty,' Theodora offered.

Richeldis kicked at an apple which turned over to reveal its rotting underside. 'If that is not an aesthetic remark, it must be a masochistic one.'

'From death comes life,' said Theodora cheerfully. After all, she'd tracked the woman to her lair. She was prepared to put in any amount of time in order to get what she wanted. If it meant prattling elementary metaphysics, her training was quite up to that.

'You've tracked me to my lair at last,' said the older woman.

'Mrs Locke Tremble seemed to suggest you wanted me to.'

'Dear Maria,' said Richeldis vaguely. 'Ever my friend. Perhaps we should go inside and get down to business.'

Without waiting for Theodora to answer, Richeldis picked up her basket and made for the French windows. 'Of course my husband's death was a huge relief. I don't deny that. Or it would be if he'd made a proper job of it.'

'He?'

'That, too, is a question. Did he intend his death or did someone else? I incline to the second theory, myself. Coffee?'

There was no alteration in Richeldis's tone as she changed from malign insinuation to domestic inquiry.

'Thank you. Black. You suspect your husband either killed himself or was killed?'

'Isn't it obvious?'

'Not to me. Not to the world. Mr Brink's announcement, the obituaries, the doctor, presumably, all agree on a heart attack.'

'Fools. Men all.' Richeldis scooped up a couple of dirty mugs from the table and disappeared through the door of the sitting room. Theodora looked round. The room resembled many she had known in her north Oxford youth. Too much mahogany furniture of a forbidding black and red patina was crowded into a small space. The chimney had been blocked up and an immense modern electric fire erected in front of it. It reminded Theodora of a nave altar moved in by a modernising priest trying to take worshippers' minds off the high altar left behind. Dark green acanthus leaves swarmed up the wall; the original William Morris wallpaper darkened an already dark room. Here was no modern decorator's Victorianising pastiche. This was pure, undisplacable inheritance. There was nothing to delight the eye or raise the spirits. Theodora had the feeling of lives lived round the furniture not in company with it. It obstructed and threatened. What would it be like, Theodora wondered, to live in despite of one's physical setting instead of with its cooperation? The only clue to Richeldis Duff's own interests was an upright piano in the corner by the window with a piano arrangement of Bach's cantatas on the stool. It was open at '*Ich habe genug*'.

'Look,' said Theodora, as Richeldis returned with

the two mugs (had she washed them?) filled with purplish looking coffee, 'if you have any doubts about the circumstances of your husband's death, surely you should see the police. My own concerns are not with that death. My only interest is in the Newcome archive, part of which, I understand from Mrs Locke Tremble, is in your care.'

Richeldis seated herself beside the unlit fire and stared into her coffee as though into a crystal ball. Perhaps she is going to practise sortilege, read the grounds, Theodora thought, scanning the weather-beaten face with its fringe of disarrayed grey hair. From Crispin's age (Theodora judged him to be seventeen or eighteen), Richeldis could not be more than in the middle fifties, but she looked ravaged and older. It was the face of a combatant who had seen action.

Richeldis ignored Theodora's invitation to talk of Newcome.

'I married Conrad because I could see no way of bettering the world except through the Church. Spiritual power is all there is, isn't it? It alone transforms.'

Theodora nodded and wondered what was coming next. She had been the recipient of many marital confidences in her time. They left her uneasy.

'The Church, as you know, doesn't really care for women. I felt marriage into the clergy might get round that.'

Theodora forebore to say she thought that was a very bad reason for marrying.

'Anyway, I'd been a music student long enough. I wasn't going to make the concert platform, so Conrad seemed a good idea. I need hardly tell you it wasn't.' Richeldis took the sounding of her coffee cup again.

'I burden you with what I'm sure is a familiar tale. I had looked for a marriage of true minds. I had a mind in those days. I am nearly sure I did. But Conrad made me doubt it. He wanted, at best, a hostess for his entertaining, at worst, a housekeeper, occasionally a nurse (he was ever prone to migraine). My understanding, my feelings, even my companionship, almost never. When he saw I could not provide the essential services, he felt he had been sold a pup and turned nasty. It was, he felt, my fault that he'd misjudged my quality.'

Richeldis took a pull at her brew. Theodora refrained.

'We started slowly,' Richeldis continued. 'I would act or speak, he would mock. He had a good line in jocoseness. He would demand, I would evade. I would converse, he would ignore me. Have you any idea how infuriating it is to ask a question and not to receive a reply, not even a glance? It dawned on me, his aim was to break my will. I was amazed at the range of his techniques and the extremes to which he would go to punish me. My survival came partly with Crispin, whose ability to annoy his father I pride myself he learnt at my knee, and partly when I discovered how ambitious Conrad was.' Richeldis paused to review the horror of her married life.

'I learned as I went on. I got better. Conrad was a good teacher, I an apt pupil. I might almost say that towards the end I had evened things up considerably.'

Theodora listened to the obsessive tone and watched the rocking to and fro of Richeldis's body as though she was engaged in some sort of obscene prayer, some incantation to free herself of her memories.

'And now,' Richeldis resumed, 'I'm damned if he's going to ruin my life or my son's or anyone else's any more. And if that means the Church is shaken to its foundations, then it has only itself to blame for preferring to high places a set of shifty hypocrites.'

'I don't follow you.'

Richeldis did not bother to look at her. 'Conrad swung both ways,' she said slowly. A smile split her mouth. 'When I found out, I thought it a rather typical manifestation of his greed. He couldn't bear that there should be pleasures that he had not tasted. But then I don't know. It might just have been power, as usual.' Richeldis ceased to smile and turned her eyes towards Theodora. 'You know what I mean?'

Theodora knew what she meant.

'Well, anyway, as time went by it seemed to me that he was beginning to give up hope, getting desperate on the career front. I was a powerful drag on him. An unsuitable wife can keep a man down in the Church of England, you know.'

Theodora knew.

'He saw paltry men preferred above him and it irked him. Then it happened.' Richeldis ceased to gaze into her coffee and fixed Theodora. 'About this time last year he got a letter from the editor of Crockford. It was an invitation to contribute the preface to the new edition, due out this year. You know its status, of course?'

'It is taken to form opinion, give a lead, even suggest policy amongst senior clergy,' Theodora admitted.

'Right.' Richeldis pressed on. 'He was very chuffed. But he didn't follow his usual ploy of boasting about it. I thought that was very odd. Normally any little success went out over the tannoy. Not, you understand, in any crude way. Just a hint here, a bit of self-deprecating boasting there.' Richeldis licked her lips.

'But the Crockford preface is anonymous,' Theodora said. 'That's why it can be outspoken, honest.' She wasn't sure which she meant.

'That never bothered Conrad. If it meant a boost to his reputation, he'd circulate the news. Well, anyway. He got the letter on a Friday, I remember. I came across it on Saturday morning. I was dusting.' Richeldis grinned virtuously at Theodora. She hardly bothered to make it convincing.

'Well, Saturday evening we were giving a party, the diocesan Bishop, a man from *The Times*, a politician who was a fellow of All Souls. The normal, careful balance. I expected the usual. But not a word.' Richeldis rubbed her horrid mug with her finger. 'I waited a week. Nothing. But Conrad was certainly working. At first I couldn't make it out. Then I found this.' Richeldis stood up and reached for a folder tucked behind the clock. She flicked it open and extracted a piece of lined A4 and handed it to Theodora.

On the paper in small, neat handwriting, in black ink, was a list of Biblical references: Exodus, Leviticus, Romans, 1 Peter. Richeldis looked up inquiringly at Theodora. Theodora gazed at it and gradually an unholy pattern began to form itself.

'Yes?' said Richeldis.

Theodora felt all the resentment of someone who is being manipulated. Why should she have to listen to this demented woman? 'Yes. I see.'

'All passages relating to sodomy. He was researching the Church's teachings on the subject from the early church down to the Bishops' last pronouncement in ninety-two.'

' "Issues in Human Sexuality". Not their finest hour in theological clarity, charity or pastoral common sense,' Theodora had to admit.

Richeldis cackled. 'You've said it. A right muddle. Well, he put in the best part of three weeks on that. Then he proceded to part two.'

'Part two?' What other horrors was this woman going to face her with? Theodora wondered.

Richeldis picked her words carefully. 'The empirical which provides the examples for the theoretical. Have I got the right words? I've learned quite a lot of the jargon over twenty years with Conrad.'

Theodora feared she might well have got the right words.

'Yes. Well. He got together a load of notes on a handful of current senior clergy; his case notes, as it were. He had a wide network. Oh, he'd been about all right. All over the place.'

'So where is the part two, the case studies?' Theodora didn't in the least want to know. She dreaded being drawn into something which would require judgements she felt unable to make or decisions she wouldn't want to execute. She felt as though the woman was deliberately tormenting her. Perhaps a tormented marriage had left Richeldis with no other pleasure.

'I don't know where the case studies are. I've hunted everywhere. They aren't amongst his papers in college or in his stuff here. I've been through them all.' She turned towards Theodora. 'Now it's up to you.'

'Why should I help you recover such information?' Richeldis smiled as one woman worker to another.

'Because if you don't, I don't think we shall discover who killed Conrad and if we don't discover that, you won't get your Newcome papers. I must say,' Richeldis continued in conversational tone, 'I do like the irony. In order to build up your hero, Newcome, you're going to have to destroy the reputation of one of his successors and with it a goodish part of the current Church of England.'

'But Crockford wouldn't publish anything scurrilous, however well evidenced.'

'They've not been too nice in the past and even if they wouldn't, other organs certainly would.'

'So what prompted him? What exactly did he say to Crockford?'

'I'm not sure he had said anything yet. But I imagine what the deal might have come down to was, get me a bishopric, or whatever it was he wanted, or I'll spill the beans.'

'But bishoprics aren't come by like that,' said Theodora.

'Yes, they are,' said Richeldis.

Theodora knew she was right. That was what the Church of England's appointment system, secretive and unaccountable, had become.

'How does this bear on Conrad Duff's death?' Theodora was prepared to leave aside the rigmarole of an unhappy and demented woman. But the fact of Conrad's death was inescapable.

'The one thing he didn't do was to commit suicide which is what Brink thinks he did.'

'Why does Brink think that?'

'Partly because of the letter. Here.' Richeldis rummaged in her file again and produced a crumpled side of plain paper. 'He was in at the death. He saw the letter. It was lying on the dresser, a single side of A4, as you see folded just once and begging to be picked up. But I got it from him,' Richeldis said with satisfaction. 'The point about having wrestled with Conrad for twenty years is that it develops the muscles. You don't fear anyone else because you know you've see the worst.'

Theodora took the paper and scanned it. The gist seemed to lie in the last line. ' "I have come to the end of my service to an institution the legitimacy of which I have come increasingly to doubt. Change and decay is all I see around me." What did he mean by that?'

'I don't think he meant anything by it. I don't think he wrote it.'

'Why not?'

'Not his typewriter face.' Richeldis oozed satisfaction. 'Conrad used a typewriter. The only one in Oxfordshire, I should think. This, however, was done on a word processor. Amstrad, by the look of it.'

'Where would there be an Amstrad?'

'Practically every student has one. They pass them on when they go down. They never seem to wear out.'

'Where was the letter?'

'On his dresser. As he lay dying,' Richeldis finished with relish.

'When did it appear there?'

'That I'd quite like you to find out.'

Another impasse, thought Theodora. Whichever way we turn, it comes down to my making inquiries.

'Why does Crispin think he was responsible for his father's death?' Theodora tried another path.

'Conrad's last words to him were, "I see you do your

97

mother's will." Naturally he interpreted that to mean I wanted his father dead.'

'Naturally.' Theodora had reached the point of no longer being surprised at Richeldis Duff's murderous thoughts. 'And I suppose Crispin is suggestible?'

'Up to now, *I* have provided the suggestions for Crispin. I was disappointed to see that his father had such an effect on him. I suppose it was the emotion of the moment. A deathbed was unfamiliar to him.'

'Mrs Locke Tremble suggested there had been some earlier altercation between Crispin and his father.'

'They bickered as always. But there was something more telling that got to Conrad that morning than a breeze with Crispin. Though, of course, Crispin wants to get away from here and Conrad is, was, adamant he should not be allowed to do so until he has some A levels and can go down the respectable paths. It's odd,' Richeldis reflected, 'what Conrad thought of as respectable.'

'But now his father is dead, he's free to pursue his own path.'

'That we shall have to work out.'

Theodora saw that having bred and schooled a son of the calibre of Crispin, Richeldis might find him difficult to place. 'Where do his tastes lie?'

'He has designs on the theatre, and Maria tells me he plays the organ quite nicely for her.'

'So if your husband did not write this suicide note, what other evidence have you that his death was not from natural causes?'

Richeldis took her time over this one. At last she said, 'His medication was missing.'

'What medication?'

'He was on something called Atroxine. If he had another heart attack he was supposed to take the stuff. He kept it always on his person. It was not with him when he had his last attack.'

Theodora reviewed her options. 'Look,' she said finally, 'if I do make some inquiries to clarify the events surrounding your husband's death, I would need to be assured about the extent and worth of the Newcome sources in your possession.'

'Perfectly fair,' said Richeldis briskly. 'Never buy a pig in a poke. Drop round tomorrow morning about ten and I'll let you have a look, just a look, mark you, at the stuff in the Newcome room.'

CHAPTER SIX

Recreation

Stephany gazed at the jumble of green letters flickering on the screen. 'What did he press, sweetie?' she asked her eldest.

Henry reflected for a moment and then pointed to the combination of numbers. 'I told Jamie not to but, you know, he doesn't really understand.' From the superiority of seven he could look on his four-year-old brother with detachment. But he was tolerant, uncensorious. Stephany loved both her sons completely. They rewarded her by liking each other. They were both generous.

About Aidan, Stephany was less sure. There were moments, especially since they had come to Gracemount, when she wondered if she really knew Dan. Part of what Stephany meant by loving someone was knowing them entirely, being able to understand and predict what they were feeling as well as what they would do. She knew her subject in that way, not just in outline or in its general principles but in precise and extended detail. She found it distressing that her pupils did not want to know all that she knew. How could they rest content with a blur of tags, quotations, half understood technical terms? If something was worth knowing, was a key to understanding how society, our world, worked, then it was surely worth knowing properly.

And now Dan, the subject on which she was an expert, was evading her, was not allowing himself to be known. For weeks they had not talked or touched. He'd not been in hall last night. When she had got back after the incident with Crispin, she'd found the boys asleep. Their supper things had been washed but not put away. There was no Dan. Sometimes Dan went walking, not, she noticed, running any more. She supposed this was to calm himself. But what did he need calming about? In their early days together in Australia at her parents' farm outside Melbourne, they had used to walk for hours together. They hadn't needed, Stephany felt, to talk because they knew what each other's thoughts were. When they did speak, it was not a surprise but a confirmation of what each already knew. And from that consolation had sprung love. At least, it had on Stephany's part. It was a great relief to her to know that others felt and perceived as she did. The youngest of three, a girl with two brothers, she knew that her intellectual abilities isolated her within the family. They were not Philistine, but they were not delicate either. To know that there were Dans in the world, in her world, who agreed with her, gave her the confidence to press on with learning.

Stephany wondered now whether she ought to have checked up on Dan. What evidence had she that their thoughts really paced side by side as their bodies had?

Dan's absence shook her. She had woken at four in the morning expecting to find him returned and beside her. Should she ring round their friends, or the local hospitals? Had he been delayed, had an accident? She feared to make a fuss, feared more to advertise to the world that anything was less than perfect between her and Dan. At six she'd risen, made tea and started to look for messages. They had no answerphone but were in the habit of leaving notes for each other by tapping into the word processor. They used the code word 'dans'. But when she tapped it in now she got this jumble of symbols and letters with no identifiable words. Frustrated, she had begun to try again when Henry padded in, wide awake and clutching his Meccano which he tended to keep on his person to work on in spare moments and also to keep it out of his brother's way.

He watched his mother cautiously for a moment before approaching. 'I'm afraid we had a bit of an accident last night,' he began. His tone, his diction, was so like Aidan's, Stephany could have wept.

'What sort of accident?' She kept her tone level so as not to alarm him.

'Well, before Dad went out, he put a message there,' he indicated the screen. 'You know, like he does.'

Stephany nodded.

'But unfortunately,' Henry got the word right so he said it again to celebrate, 'unfortunately, Jamie got at it.'

'You were both supposed to be in bed.'

Henry looked a bit guilty. 'I had an idea about my palace.' He tapped his Meccano construct. 'So I thought I'd better just try it out before I forgot.'

'I thought it was a boat,' Stephany said, her attention momentarily tugged from her own wider troubles.

Henry looked pained. 'No. I told you. It's a palace.'

'Henry, in what order did Jamie press the keys. I mean what did he press first?'

Henry looked unhappy. 'He started at the top and then just dabbed about a bit.'

Stephany shook her head. 'He's scrambled the message entirely. I can't make it out.'

'Scrambled the message.' Henry liked the scrambled bit. 'Scrambled like eggs?' he enquired.

'Like eggs,' said Stephany sadly.

'Where's Dad?' Henry pursued.

Scrambled, Stephany was tempted to say and didn't. There was no point in placing her misery on Henry's shoulders. 'He'll be back soon. He left a message, after all.'

The stables in the Sunday afternoon calm smelt of sweet hay and sweetly rotting manure. The yard's paving of black bricks was warm under the October sun. Two bays, their heads propped on the door of their boxes, their eyes hooded, failed to hear Theodora as she walked slowly round the three sides of the square towards the door marked 'office'. As she laid a hand on it, all hell broke loose. Theodora's ear detected at least one soprano Jack Russell, a bass Alsatian and something a bit between the two, a baritone, perhaps a Springer. It was as if a spell of enchantment had been broken. Where all had been peace, now a tractor roared into life behind the stable block and at the same moment a car drove into the yard and screeched to a halt outside the office door. From it emerged a vaguely familiar figure beautifully turned out in immaculate cream breeches, well-fitting brown check jacket, brown top boots and brown hard hat. It was the earrings which identified the figure.

'Mrs Gainley,' said Theodora with pleasure.

'Ha,' said Mrs Gainley, looking over Theodora's darned greyish jodhpurs and short boots like a Guide captain reviewing her troop. 'I wouldn't open that door, if I were you. The Sach and the Springer wouldn't hurt a fly but the Jack Russell's an absolute beggar. Gets right through leather with no trouble at all.'

Theodora took her hand off the door knob. Mrs Gainley glanced again at what she clearly considered Theodora's inadequate trim. 'Looking for Joyce, are you?'

'I thought I might just see if they would let me have something to hack out on.'

'Research not going too well?'

'I've met a bit of a block,' Theodora admitted. 'Too many strands.' Theodora was disingenuous. Providence had placed Mrs Gainley in her path. She might as well test out one or two points.

'Nothing like the back of a horse for restoring a proper perspective. How much have you done?'

Theodora understood the question referred to her standard of horsemanship. 'I don't think I'd hurt anything in the heavy hunter line.'

Mrs Gainley seemed to come to a conclusion. 'I'll get Joyce and we'll see what we can do. I keep an old bay here,' she nodded in the direction of the previously slumbering bays, 'and if you don't object to Hovis and me, we could hack round the park together. I don't think they'd let someone without form go out on their own first time.'

Theodora was aware of the favour. 'That would be very agreeable.'

Mrs Gainley stood on tiptoe, found a length of rope hanging down beside the office door and tugged. The sound of the bell set the dogs' chorus off again.

'Yes,' said a voice from the other side of the yard. 'What is it? Oh, it's you, Thelma.' A tall woman, handsome as her charges and with a long nose as though in sympathy with them, strode across the bricks. 'The wind's going to change to the north-west and it'll be raining before evening. Then we've got a cold front coming over from Norway, the Farmers says,' she offered by way of greeting.

'I didn't catch it.'

'It's the only reliable one.'

'Oh, I know.'

Theodora was interested to see Mrs Gainley, so downright and assured in her own sphere, positively deferential to Joyce.

'Joyce knows all there is to know about weather.' Mrs Gainley reflected pride in her friend's ability. 'Joyce, this is an old friend of mine, Miss Braithwaite. Mrs Challenger.'

Mrs Challenger looked over Theodora's left shoulder as though reading the clouds. But Theodora took this to be a not unfriendly gesture.

'Miss Braithwaite was wondering if you could mount her. Just for a quiet walk round the park,' Mrs Gainley hurried on.

'Staying at Gracemount?'

'Just for the week.'

'How much have you done?'

Theodora repeated her line about heavy hunters.

106

'She's pretty competent,' Mrs Gainley chipped in. Theodora was amused to see her backing what could only be a very dark horse on the basis of a mere twenty-four hours' acquaintance.

'She could have Rummy,' Mrs Gainley suggested, still deferential.

Joyce glared across the yard at the smaller of the two bays who by this time had altered his expression from sleepy to hungry-hopeful. He was biting the top of his door in a desultory way.

'Spooks a bit,' said Joyce.

'Many do,' Theodora agreed.

Her answer seemed to convince Joyce. Once decided, she and Mrs Gainley got things together quickly. The surprised and resentful Rummy was tacked up and led out while Mrs Gainley brought her own darker bay up to the mounting block. Hovis was a good seventeen hands; Mrs Gainley was a small woman. A feat like mountaineering took place while she placed a foot firmly in the middle of his ribs and hauled herself up his side and into the saddle.

'Had to back you,' Mrs Gainley flung over her shoulder as they walked out in single file down the lane towards the village street. 'Otherwise Joyce wouldn't have come across.'

'I'm very much obliged,' said Theodora.

'Well, I'm a good judge of horseflesh.' Mrs Gainley was complacent. 'And, to be honest, I have my reasons. One or two matters I'd like to discuss.'

Theodora thought of all the matters she, too, would like to discuss and how very difficult that was going to be, conversing at the tops of their voices, one behind the other. But they continued out of the lane into the road with no sign of Mrs Gainley allowing her to draw abreast. 'Have you been round the estate?' she inquired.

'Only the bits I could do walking. The path up to the Hermes pond, for example.' Then she wondered if this label would mean anything to Mrs Gainley. It was, after all, only owing to Newcome's own writing that she called it by this name.

'The one leading to the round pond? Why Hermes?'

'Henry Newcome called it that in a diary of his. His wife, Esther, gave him a figure of Hermes for the middle. But it's no longer there.'

'Wouldn't be the first naked man that grove's seen,' Mrs Gainley opined.

Theodora thought it safer in all senses to get alongside Mrs Gainley. As she drew level, the two bays put their ears back, slid their eyes under them and made simultaneous attempts to bite each other's necks.

'Stop making faces,' Mrs Gainley chided her huge animal with affectionate pride. Theodora concentrated on her seat bones to catch the rhythm of Rummy's walk which was not unbalanced though a trifle lethargic.

'What I mean to say is,' Mrs Gainley went on, 'I think it's high time we had a bit of a clear-up.'

Theodora waited. The horses settled with irritation for each other's company. As long as Theodora kept Rummy's head slightly behind Hovis, Hovis apparently felt he was winning and so could tolerate his stable companion. Theodora thought how very human horses were and how what was unlovable in human beings was perfectly acceptable in horses. Was it the fur that made all the difference?

'I mean Aidan Prior has left home. Crispin Duff is

having one of his turns and Matthew Brink is looking for something which he can't find.'

'What do you mean about Dan?' Theodora saw no reason to disguise her astonishment.

'Left yesterday evening. Wasn't in hall. Saw him shoot off on his bike down the drive just as we were delivering Crispin back to his mama. Bike isn't back in the shed, ergo . . .'

'I thought, I mean . . .' Theodora was at a loss. 'Stephany never mentioned . . .' Then Theodora thought, I haven't seen Stephany today. She hadn't been at the college Communion this morning. 'Why has Dan gone and where?'

'It was an Oxford number.'

'What?'

'He came into Bishop's House last night just before hall. There's a public phone for students' use outside my office. It's an old-fashioned dial affair. I can tell you all the codes round here by the sound. Oxford, London, Reading, Buckingham. Oxford sounds like . . .' Mrs Gainley took her left hand off the rein and conducted herself through the sounds made by 01865. Hovis put his ears back in case he needed to listen, decided he didn't and pointed them forward again.

Theodora was impressed. 'What about the rest of the number?'

'I didn't get it. I was changing into my glad rags at the time to come down to hall and it wasn't until I came out of my office and saw it was Aidan that I had any interest.' Mrs Gainley was honest.

'Why do you think he's left home?'

'It's been building up since the Warden's death.'

'What has?'

'Dan was very close to Conrad Duff.'

'So Stephany said.'

'Did she? Well, I suppose Conrad never bothered to mind people's feelings. Of course, it caused a lot of bother. We could take a trot here if you felt like it.' They had turned out of the lane into the main street of the village. The sharp rattle of horses' hooves on the hard surface lifted all their spirits. Rummy gave a couple of shuddering coughs and then settled for a pleasant, balanced, forward-going pace which matched Hovis's stiffer gait. They cleared the road and the bridge and made for the rise which would lead them into the woods of Gracemount.

'What sort of bother?'

'Matt Brink had been chief lord in waiting to the Warden until Aidan and Stephany came on the scene.' Mrs Gainley had no problem in resuming her line of thought.

'And Brink didn't care for that?'

'Dan was acting more or less as Conrad's secretary toward the end. Matt Brink had known Conrad for twenty years. Watched him rise. Admired him. You know how men do.'

Theodora stored this away for later reflection. Did women follow each other's careers or marriages as proprietorially?

'So Brink was resentful, jealous even of Dan?'

'He was edgy with him. Patronising, a bit jocose. We turn here.'

'That isn't reason enough for Dan to leave home surely.'

'My bet is that Dan left home because he knows who killed Conrad Duff.'

Theodora didn't have time to respond to this interesting idea. Rummy, on the outside of the pair, glimpsed a pile of hedge clippings which certainly hadn't been there last time he'd come this way. They reminded him strongly of snakes. Also there was the question of delayed tea. He spun round within his own length, took canter and made back for the stable. Theodora pushed her right knee down and kept the left hand, cursing herself for not having got him together earlier. She half halted him (not that he noticed) and managed to turn him. She took trot, did not rise, took walk and turned him through a ten-metre circle on the right rein. Then she straightened him through a couple of paces, changed the rein and turned him through a left-hand circle just to show who was boss. Before he realised what had come over him he was on the bit and walking securely past the clippings. Foiled of his plan, he rejoined Hovis who had been halted to observe the pantomine.

'Very nice,' said Mrs Gainley. 'I knew I was a judge of horseflesh.'

'You were saying something about the Warden's death,' Theodora said, not relenting for an instant and keeping Rummy a couple of inches shorter than he thought was fair.

'Matt and Richeldis think it's suicide. But I have my doubts.'

'Why?'

'They think it was because of the letter.'

How much Thelma Gainley seemed to know, Theodora thought. Richeldis was under the impression that she and Brink alone knew about the letter.

'It was lying about for days on Conrad's desk in his

study at home. Then it turned up on his dressing table
when he lay dying. If you're going to write a suicide
note, you don't leave it in your in tray.'

'How do you know it lay about for days?'

'Crispin told me.'

It occurred to Theodora to wonder how reliable
Crispin was as a witness. On the other hand, why
should he lie? 'When you say it was in his study, you
mean his study in his apartment, not his study across
the hall, his college room?'

'Right. What came on to his desk in the Warden's
room in college, I would know all about. The annoying
thing was that he did his scholarly stuff in his study
at home. That I didn't always know about.'

Theodora found this an interesting reflection on the
work habits of both Conrad and Mrs Gainley.

'You're in Crispin's confidence then?'

'My brother is Justin Pinkrose,' said Mrs Gainley.

'TV director, actor,' Theodora said out of imperfectly
remembered newspaper reports.

'Something like that,' Mrs Gainley said dourly,
shifting in the saddle. 'We don't get on. Chalk and
cheese. But sometimes he uses me as a refuge when
he wants to hide out from his creditors. And Crispin
met him last time he was down. He's nuts to go on the
TV, is young Crispin. I'm worth cultivating from that
point of view. Anyway, I'm sorry for the lad. Though I
can't say I think acting's any job for a man.'

'The idea of a great TV actor . . .' Theodora ventured.

'Self-contradictory,' Mrs Gainley agreed.

'So this letter,' Theodora brought her back.

'I usually give Hovis a bit of a stretch out round
about here,' said Mrs Gainley, nodding towards the

broad ride through the trees which would, on
Theodora's calculation, bring them round to the far
side of Gracemount.

The going was good to soft. The beech leaves were
thick on the ground and the path not apparently much
used. Rummy did his overture of coughs which shook
him from nose to dock and then, in the face of
Theodora's firm leg and hand, settled into quite a
smooth canter. Cautiously she lifted her weight for
the saddle and took it on to her knees and thus in
comfort and accord they belted after the huge figure
of Hovis who had thrown himself forward into a
powerful gallop, his long legs eating up the ground.
Rummy, who was quite short-coupled and not a slouch,
kept him in sight. At the end of the track, Mrs Gainley
drew rein. Theodora came up in good order and
together they gazed through coppiced chestnuts towards the north facade of Gracemount.

'So this letter, the suicide note, you think it was
not genuine in some way.'

'As I said, according to Crispin it had been hanging
around his desk at home. Anyway, Conrad wasn't
suicidal. Murderous perhaps. Well, I mean,' Mrs
Gainley caught herself up, 'he caused others to be
unhappy.'

'Richeldis? Crispin?'

'He wasn't kind to either. He treated Brink like a
dog. He was a mischief maker. He liked a posse of
people round him in attendance – Brink, Wade, Dan,
Spin even. And he liked to play them off against each
other.'

Theodora knew about the admiring clique. What
she needed to know more precisely was why, apart

from the falsity of the suicide letter, Mrs Gainley should think that the Warden had been killed and why she should suppose that Dan knew who had done it. She was aware of a degree of immediate self-interest. She wanted to have something to offer Richeldis to act as a bribe or a lever to allow her to bargain for access to the Newcome papers tomorrow morning.

'So why don't you think the Warden died of a heart attack? The doctor thought he did.' Theodora remembered Richeldis's remarks about the absent medication. How much did Mrs Gainley really know about the health of Conrad Duff?

'Look.' Mrs Gainley half turned in her saddle and let out the rein the better to allow Hovis to crop the thin grass at his feet. 'The morning he died, absolutely everyone was there. You'd think in the vac there'd be no one about in college,' Mrs Gainley mused, 'but actually, the moment term ends and the students go, we instantly get much matier. More relaxed and so on. People dress differently, fewer clerical collars. Well, anyway, the day Conrad died was hot. Doors and windows open. You could hear voices over longish distances. For instance, from where I sit in my little office, I heard Ellenor Spin look in on Richeldis earlyish, about nine thirty.'

'I wouldn't have thought the two would be friends.'

'They weren't. But Ellenor gets Richeldis her sleeping stuff. I think it's off prescription. Anyway, they both carry on as though it's contraband. They both like a mystery. Then,' Mrs Gainley was clearly getting to the heart of the matter, 'Brink came in to see Conrad at about ten.' She stopped and they listened to the sound of the horses searching for grass amongst the leaves. 'You know Conrad was on drugs for his heart?'

Theodora nodded. Get on with it.

'When he had his attack the bottle of stuff wasn't with him.'

'What do you mean "not with him"?'

'He was supposed to keep them with him, in his pocket, in case of an attack. When he had his attack that day, they weren't with him.'

'How do you know?'

'Because I saw them somewhere else.'

'Where?'

'By half past eleven they were in Matthew Brink's in tray.'

'But how?'

'I went in for some stuff he was supposed to let me have. Matthew never has anything on time. He tries but he doesn't get there. Well, I went in about half eleven. He wasn't there. I thought the stuff might be in his tray so I rifled through. Halfway down I found the Atroxine bottle.'

Theodora thought about this. Was it true and if so what did it mean? 'You're saying Brink removed the medication from Conrad Duff, in the hope or the expectation that he'd have an attack and die from its lack.'

'It might not have been him who actually removed the medication.' Mrs Gainley was cautious. 'Anyone could have removed it and slipped it in amongst Matt's things. What I'm saying is that on the day of Conrad's death there were plenty of people about.'

'How many people knew Duff was on medication?'

'The group all knew.'

'The group?'

'Conrad's clique. Brink, Spin, Wade, Dan, and, of course, his family, Richeldis and Crispin.'

'And you.'

'And me.'

'And you reckon Dan knows who took the medication off Duff and therefore who killed him.'

'Yes.'

'And Dan can't cope with that knowledge.'

'Right.'

'Why not?'

Mrs Gainley thought for a moment. 'I reckon it damages someone he cares about.'

'And who does he care about?'

'I think he cares about his family,' said Mrs Gainley after reflection. 'But his buddy, after Conrad, was Wade.'

'Well, it can't be both Wade and Brink who killed Conrad,' Theodora objected. 'And Wade in any case didn't arrive on the scene until Conrad was dead. Quite apart from the absence of motive. I mean, why should they or anyone want to kill Conrad?'

'Ah, there you have scope for your talents.'

'So what's to be done?' Theodora asked.

Mrs Gainley smiled encouragingly. 'I thought you might care to put nose to trail.'

'Why should I?'

'Look,' said Mrs Gainley, 'I think I mentioned we've got a visitation on Wednesday. The Bishop and the Archdeacon are coming down to sort out the succession. To take soundings. To tell us how we're placed. Or whatever. You know and I know there are too many theological colleges. It only takes Crispin or Richeldis to say one of your clergy murdered my husband stroke

116

father, or indeed to say my distinguished father stroke husband, whatever, committed suicide, for the place to be finished. Do you want that, Miss Braithwaite? You're writing a life of its founder, you must feel for the place.'

Theodora was surprised at the strength of Mrs Gainley's emotion. She thought of the long tradition of training priests. She thought, too, of the scandals which seemed to have beset every aspect of the Church in recent years. Each diminished its influence, reduced its credibility as an institution capable of giving spiritual and moral leadership to the world. Its virtues were unsung and quiet, its faults made headlines. Then, too, there was the question of justice. Whatever Conrad Duff had or had not done, his death did not, ought not to have rested in any man's hand.

'So you think someone, me, ought to try to find out the truth.'

'What I think is,' Mrs Gainley changed tack, tapping her toe against her horse's side and hauling in the rein to bring a reluctant head with it, 'that the whole joy of riding is that to do it successfully you have to do exactly the opposite of what you're taught to do in every other sphere of life. Try a bit harder, strive, exert yourself, push, pull, is what we're taught, isn't it? If you do any of that on a horse you'll come off. A sort of relaxed alertness is the clue to success in riding. As you yourself know, Miss Braithwaite.'

'Got your knitting?'

'Got your New Testament Greek's more to the point, my lad.' Rita organised Trevor just the way he liked.

'Yep, all present and correct.'

Rita stretched up to ring the bell on the Priors' flat. 'Hello, love,' she said to Henry.

Henry had used both hands to open the door and continued to hold on to it as he swung it open. He looked at her gravely.

'Who is it, Henry?' Stephany's voice from the interior sounded muffled.

'Rita and Trevor,' said Henry not turning round.

'Who?'

'It's us.'

Stephany appeared behind her son. 'Oh, I'd forgotten.'

This was not like Stephany. 'Have we got it wrong?'

'No. No, you're quite right. Come in. I'm sorry. I . . .'

It occurred to Rita that Stephany had been crying. 'Look, if there's been a change of arrangements, that's quite all right by Trev and me.'

'Quite OK,' said Trevor who saw his supper disappearing.

The living room which was usually so neat had piles of unfiled stuff lying about. On the table, where supper ought to have been laid, were books, on chairs washing, on the floor the litter of Henry's Meccano.

'We, I, Dan and me were going to supper with the Spins. But I, we, had to cancel.' Stephany seemed at a loss. 'Dan's been called away suddenly.' She did not sound convincing.

'Nothing wrong, I hope?' Rita's honest social worker's eye took it all in. Stephany had spent the entire day waiting for Dan to ring and playing with the computer to try to recover his message.

'Stay and have a bite.' In her troubles Stephany's Australian accent was prominent.

'That'd be right nice.' Trevor nipped in before Rita could consult her conscience or her manners or whatever else it was that stood in the way of all the pleasures of life which Trevor clearly saw no reason not to partake of.

'Can I stay up too?' Henry reckoned that the way he'd had to cope with his mother today, it was the least of his desserts.

Stephany smiled. She'd got to make the best. They were in the hands of Providence. Dan would call. She only had to have patience. 'Yes, all right. Rita, could you give me a hand? Jamie's been done. He's in bed. It's just us.'

'Trevor'll clear the place up a bit,' said Rita halfway to the kitchen.

The domestic dance sedated Stephany's misery. Rita was so very competent. She had all the skills. I bet she can make marmalade, Stephany thought to herself as she and Rita assembled the meal. It was Stephany's private touchstone of home-making virtue. Hers never set. The shared tasks brought intimacy, otherwise Stephany would never have uttered her worries.

'The point is,' she said as she peeled parsnips and Rita chopped onions at a rate of knots, 'I don't know where Dan is. Not right now.'

Rita was too experienced to show any large reaction. 'Oh, aye.' She scooped onions (why did they not make her cry? Stephany paused to wonder) into a frying pan.

'He left a message on the word processor.'

Rita cast her a glance.

'When we first got one, Aidan didn't like it and wasn't using it to its full potential.' The old Stephany the tutor showed through. 'So I made him use it for domestic messages.'

'You've got to teach them,' Rita agreed, referring, Stephany understood, to mankind in general.

'Well, last night Jamie got to the machine first and scrambled the message Dan put on before he went. So now I just don't know...'

Rita proceeded to treat the carrots in the same way as the onions. 'Oh, Trev'll recover it for you,' she said equably. 'Even Amstrad's memories never entirely disappear. He's quite a dab hand when it comes to retrieval, is our Trev. Let him have a go after supper.'

CHAPTER SEVEN

Victorian Life

'You've got an hour, Ma says.'

'Thank you.' Theodora eyed Crispin. The wind had changed to the north-west, there was rain in the air. It had turned colder. Crispin wore a whitish running singlet and a pair of black practice tights. It struck Theodora that Crispin had been underdressed on all the occasions she had met him.

'I'll collect you.' Crispin showed signs of lingering. Theodora had no time to spare for Crispin. As the college chapel struck ten, she had presented herself at the Warden's apartment, notebook in hand. She had had to wait before she got a response. Now all she wanted was to get to Newcome's papers.

'Thank you,' she repeated firmly to Crispin and instantly felt remorse. He was surely the sort of youth people were always shutting out, shaking off, evading. No wonder he took to acting in public. Perhaps when, if, he ever had a legitimate audience all his own, his histrionic urge would be satisfied.

Crispin did a slow dissolve from the door and

Theodora surveyed the room. It was a hexagonal turret room with two windows, one looking west, the other north. Consequently at this time of day and season it was sunless. One shutter on the north window had been thrown back, otherwise the room was in Victorian gloom. There was a central gas mantle which lacked shades. She must remember to bring a torch. The floor was bare of carpet but the boards at some time had been stained and waxed as though this should suffice. Against the wall next to the door was the only piece of furniture, a desk over which, just at eye level, hung an Italianate crucifix in brass and marble. At the desk stood a single, upright chair inviting, waiting. Round every other wall were bookshelves tightly packed with books. The room had the air, common to many rooms inhabited by strong personalities, of waiting for his or her return, of accepting nothing less than the owner. Turret rooms in fairy stories are centres of magic and revelation but Theodora felt she intruded.

She also saw, looking at the book stock, that it would need days, months of work to go through the shelves. How much of the stuff was Newcome's, how much subsequent wardens? Well, there had been only four since Newcome died. But still, she would need to sort out his library from others and from his personal papers. Then she would need to decide how much of his personal library she would have to read in addition to his own papers. She knew the period. She'd read the relevant theology. But there was always the danger that she might have missed just that author who meant most to Thomas Henry himself. She knew from experience that it is not always the person we quote from most who is our greatest influence. It is as though we do not wish to share but to keep private, secret even, whoever is most precious to us. To admit we have learned our wisdom from another source is to admit our vulnerability.

The thing to do was to prioritise. The diaries for 1879, the year immediately before the publication of *Cities of Men*, were surely her first concern. She ran her eye over the dusty shelves, discarding the reference texts, Westcott and Hort, Hastings, the Latin and Greek fathers in Italian and Spanish editions. Where would the personal stuff be shelved? At the far end of the north wall, the unvarying orderliness gave place to a jumble of slim black volumes with loose papers bulging out of them. Taking a prudent duster from her briefcase, Theodora eased them from their place. The dust spun itself into skeins when she spread the diaries out on the desk. The loose papers interleaved between the pages were letters. Theodora smoothed out the first of them. It was on thick, cream, matt paper written in a firm, beautiful copperplate.

It is not the least of the advantages of our new situation that it affords us the opportunity to hear modern music of the first quality. Last evening, as it fell out, we were at the Standevens in Chester Gate and Frederick had taken a box for Herr Weber's new operatic work, Die Freischutz. *Nothing would satisfy him but that Thomas and I should accompany them and, though I had hardly the 'tenue' for such an occasion, we were most happy to be persuaded.*

I cannot tell you, dearest Emma, with what delight we heard those sublime sounds which seemed to reach into our innermost depths and raise from them the most noble feelings of which we are capable. We got home to Gracemount a little before the midnight hour, just as Thomas had foretold, our new railway line being a most convenient blessing, and John met us with the new pony who goes to his work with such 'brio' that the journey did not take us above a quarter of an hour. So you see, such are the pleasures which open to us in our new abode where you will, I hope, my dearest sister, join us as soon as Papa's health allows.

The note was signed 'Your loving sister, Esther' and dated December 12th, 1878. Not for the first time Theodora wondered what made families keep that sort of trivia clogging up the arteries of scholarship. Hang it, it wasn't Esther and her domestic details she wanted to know about. It was her husband's more profound thought that she wanted to track. But as she turned the letters over she began gradually to revise her estimate of Esther. Some of the earliest dated letters were from the period before her marriage to Thomas Henry. Detained in spite of herself by the quality of the writing and the liveliness of the personality which emerged, Theodora read on.

As she turned the pages, Theodora wondered why she had supposed that so distinguished a man as Thomas Henry Newcome would choose a silly wife. Victorian society was replete with women whose qualities and achievement overtopped our own more lackadaisical age. They'd had to strive, we have it easy by comparison, Theodora reflected. It was clear that before her marriage Esther had moved in the first circles of London intellectual society. In her father's house in Streatham, she'd met some of the best minds of her time. The Leweses had dined. Chapman had supped. Mrs Oliphant had taken tea. Trollope had dashed in and out. Esther's father, the Reverend Standforth Chalfont, had been a Unitarian minister of great repute. Esther Chalfont, the elder of his two daughters, turned out to be at twenty, the year before her marriage to Newcome, a busier, cleverer woman than Theodora had supposed. She not only went about, she read and reflected on what she read. She had returned the year before from eighteen months with a Protestant family in 'Bruxelles', as Esther called it. Theodora read her entry for January 1866. Here were her views on the woman question dated to the year before her marriage in 1867. She had been taken to a lecture given by Frau Bannman and returned unimpressed.

Mr Trollope said she was ridiculous and she was. I never saw such a frump and her views so very unyielding. Surely it cannot be conducive to marital harmony for women to be always longing to take the commanding positions of men? And if we spend our time longing and working for this end, is there not a great danger that we may at last succumb to imitating their vices rather than emulating their virtues?

Hell's teeth, Theodora thought. She'd have to do some more work on Esther; much more work than she had time for. She saw her completion date moving further and further into the future. The only good thing was that she had not tried to line up a publisher who would be breathing down her neck for the finished product. At the very least she must find space in her biography to give Esther her due.

She turned over the pages and sorted them from the diaries. System was rewarded. Once free of the interleaved letters, most of which seemed to be from Esther to her sister, the diaries emerged in good order and clearly dated. They started in January 1879, the missing year.

They were, Theodora thought, as she carefully turned page after closely written page, all that she could wish. Newcome was an assiduous diarist. What was the urge which precipitated the writing of diaries? she wondered. Was it to catch the moment, in an age before photography became usual? Or was it to commune with one's own soul when it was not safe to share that thinking with another? Or was it to give shape to the chaos of experience and assure ourselves thereby of its significance? It was a fact, as far as Theodora could see, that the diaries of writers were a good deal less interesting than their published works. The trivia was strained off in the diary, leaving the quality and substance to be used in the published work. But with Newcome this was not quite true. He used his diary to refine his thinking. Into the daily record of his affairs were intercalated extracts from his reading, thoughts on his spiritual life, prayers, notes for sermons. And running though all was the clearly marked drafts of what she recognised would finally form the structure of *Cities of Men*.

There were three volumes. It would take at least a

week to read them, never mind assimilate and relate them to the published text of *Cities of Men*. She looked at her watch. She had fifteen minutes to the hour. She cursed Mrs Duff, Conrad Duff, their son, the whole contemporary Gracemount establishment. What right had they to keep her from her find? What were their pretty concerns and problems compared to Newcome's vision of the Church and society? Who cared whether Duff had died by his own hand or been done to death by someone else?

Theodora caught herself up. Of course it mattered. What, in the first place, was the Church other than its members? And what was a vision compared to the demands of a present reality? If something was badly wrong at Gracemount now and it involved, for example, Aidan and Stephany or even the pitiable Crispin, and his rancorous mother, then that must be her immediate duty. She must see what sort of deal she could strike with Richeldis.

She piled the diaries on to the desk in the hope of an early return to them and turned her mind to the problems of Gracemount as offered to her through the perspectives of Mrs Gainley, Maria Locke Tremble, Richeldis Duff, Mrs Spin, Aidan and Stephany.

Stephany had been her first port of call last night after she'd parted from Thelma Gainley. Her words about Dan not being in hall and not being about since struck her conscience. Why hadn't she sought Stephany out when she'd not been in college Communion? She had to admit she'd wanted to track down Richeldis and not let her friendship with Aidan and Stephany take up too much of her precious time. When she finally got to Stephany and Aidan's flat, she'd found

Rita and Trevor and an air of partying. Rita was putting Henry to bed. Stephany and Trevor were drinking wine and mutually congratulating each other in front of Aidan's ancient word processor in the study.

'Dan's with Tim Wade,' Stephany had burst out the minute she walked through the door, as though Theodora already knew all about his absence.

'Stephany was a bit worried because Jamie'd lost his message on the PC,' Trevor said. He liked to be of use. He felt it equalled up his relationship with the womenfolk, so he was happy.

It was on the tip of Theodora's tongue to ask what Dan was doing at Wade's but she saw the relief on Stephany's face and bit it back.

Stephany said, 'I guess he'll ring when he's ready. He and Tim knew Conrad Duff very well.'

She seemed to think this settled matters.

Now, twelve hours later with time to ponder, Theodora did wonder what was going on with Duff's retinue. Crispin proclaimed he had killed his father. His mother wanted Theodora to find out someone else who was responsible. Brink apparently thought it was suicide. Did Wade think the same? Mrs Locke Tremble thought along with Richeldis. Mrs Gainley thought it was murder and her evidence, if true, seemed to implicate Brink in some way. What did Dan think? Did Mrs Spin have an opinion or indeed knowledge? And what was their evidence? Brink had seen a letter which he took to be a suicide note from Conrad, Richeldis had said. Mrs Gainley was sure the letter wasn't a real suicide note because it had been 'hanging about' Conrad's papers for some time. Richeldis also thought the note was false because it was done on a word processor whereas Conrad habitually used a typewriter. Mrs Locke Tremble thought he had been killed 'because he had many enemies'. What would that mean? That he had been blackmailing someone? Well, according to Richeldis, Conrad was blackmailing the editor of Crockford and the whole Anglican establishment. Then there was the question of method. Richeldis thought her husband had been killed because, when his heart had failed, he lacked his salvatory medicine. According to Mrs Gainley that medicine was in Brink's in tray. But how about if it had been suicide? Was Conrad Duff the type? On the whole the verdict seemed to be that Conrad had much to live for at the very moment when he was taken. If his Crockford move came off, it might mean that prize of preferment, which he so ardently desired, was at last going to slide into his hands.

Theodora got up and moved across the bare room to the north window. She eased the casement and cool air rushed in. Far away in the valley below the sun lit up the brown beech trees. In the face of beauty, how could she not feel that all would be well? 'If someone did kill Conrad Duff,' Theodora found herself speaking aloud, 'why not let it be? Why not leave it to Providence?'

' "Vengeance is mine, saith the Lord, I will pursue," ' came the reply.

Theodora swung round and found herself facing Richeldis.

'No murderer, no Newcome sources,' said Richeldis. 'Surely you, as a priest – no? A deacon then, can't let the world be polluted by an unsolved crime. Both justice and ambition move you in that direction.'

Theodora cursed the woman for her acuteness.

'You want to make your name as Newcome's biographer, Miss Braithwaite. Is that not so?'

'I think a clearer understanding of his life and work could help us to see what the Church can do for society at the present time. A good biography might do that.'

'How you cloak your own ambition is not my concern. Personally, I think the whole edifice could come down and no one would miss it.'

Theodora, desperate to convince this implacable woman, tried to keep her tone level. 'But we aren't even sure that there has been a crime committed. He may just have died from heart failure.'

Richeldis went on as though she had not heard her. 'There is, too, the question of my unhappy son's self-accusation.'

'Why does Crispin think he killed his father?'

'There had been,' Richeldis said carefully, 'as I said, an altercation.'

'Between Conrad and Crispin?'

Richeldis nodded. 'I didn't, on this occasion, actually join in. Crispin has got to learn to keep his end up. But I expect it was the same old subject. It had been going on for weeks. A levels. Careers. Conrad, one of the most consummate performers who ever drew breath, despised the stage, the screen. No son of his was going to waste his time in such a milieu. I surmise it reached a head that morning. Decisions had to be made. Application forms and so on. Conrad wouldn't listen, Crispin kept on refusing.'

'Crispin fears the quarrel may have contributed to the heart attack?'

'Their spats were too frequent for them to have any

effect on Conrad. Conrad liked fighting provided it was from a superior position. Though they took it out of Crispin. No stamina,' she said with the contempt of the seasoned campaigner for the tyro. 'No, as you know, what killed Conrad in my view was one of two things. Either someone who knew challenged him about part two of his Crockford preface or someone who knew deprived him of his medicine.'

'Who knew about the preface?'

'That's for you to find out.'

'And would that be the same person who deprived him of Atroxine?'

'That's for you to find out.'

Theodora restrained her irritation. There was an interesting point here about final causes. Richeldis, she judged, was in no mood to examine it.

'Well now, Miss Braithwaite, what about this stuff of Newcome's? Do you want it or not?'

'Yes,' said Theodora, making her decision. 'There's a great deal of very valuable material here. Indeed, no biography could be written without it.'

'So you accept my terms?'

'I suspect you've no legal right to keep Newcome's archive from me. It must be part of the Newcome estate which Thomas Henry left to the college.'

'I should, of course, contest that on every point,' said Richeldis suavely. 'And even should you win, it will take you time and money. Have you got either of those, Miss Braithwaite?'

'You know I haven't.'

'So?'

'Very well.' Theodora felt she had lost morally as well as practically.

'So it's a deal, you'll get Conrad's killer?' Richeldis's unwinking eye and thin moist lips regarded Theodora as though she was something tasty to eat. She doesn't care about her husband's killer, Theodora thought. I'm not even sure her son is her first concern. What she wants is Conrad's part two material so she can use it to damage the Church.

'I'll find out what I can about the circumstances of your husband's death. However, if there is a case for murder, I shall turn it over to the police which, in my view, you should do at once.'

'We'll see what it is you unearth first,' said Richeldis.

'I'll need a timetable of events on the day of your husband's death.' Theodora was reminded of her similar task vis-à-vis Newcome's biography. Biographies had to have linear narrative. They all assumed *post hos ergo propter hoc*. Such a banausic view.

'Give me time,' said Richeldis. 'I'll write down what I can remember and let you have it. I'll get it to you after lunch.'

Theodora thought, she's enjoying power. Years with Conrad Duff have taught her how to use it.

'When,' Theodora asked, 'can I return to the Newcome sources?'

Richeldis considered. 'I wouldn't want to be unfair. Say you have Newcome in the morning and I have your time for the afternoons.'

Theodora thought they might have been negotiating a cleaning contract. 'Yes, all right.'

'And I need hardly remind you of the time constraint. I want everything in order by the time the trustees visit the day after tomorrow, Wednesday. If they think they're going to keep this lot going, I want something to force their hands. Gracemount has done nothing but harm. Giving people like Conrad the care of the young, entrusting him with the formation of priests when he can't even form his own son, is culpable.'

'But . . .' Theodora was at a loss for words. Did she agree or not? She wasn't sure. How else could you train priests, particularly priests who valued the catholic tradition? She simply hadn't thought of alternatives.

'So you see, Miss Braithwaite,' Richeldis brought her face uncomfortably close to Theodora's, 'either way, this place has had it.'

'The function of religion in society is to provide a focus for people's good instincts and a set of practices to help us cope with our darker ones. The Hebrew word for instinct is?' Stephany looked round at her class.

No one was going to make a fool of themselves over this one.

'*Yetzer*,' Stephany supplied. 'In Rabbinic thought every human being has two of them. A good *yetzer* and a bad *yetzer*. So powerful are these instincts that we give them supernatural status and project them on to the world outside us. All societies have gods and devils.'

Isaiah Ngaio copied this down quickly in his clear schoolteacher's hand. He knew all the words but somehow it just didn't make sense. Things had got the wrong way round. It was as though man was speaking about God, but surely theology was about God speaking to man. He had grown increasingly puzzled by this tilt in his studies. However, he had examinations to pass and he wasn't going to quarrel with the lecturer. Perhaps if he waited a bit all would become clear. To his right Trevor gazed out of the window and thought it would be a good day for hockey.

Stephany looked round her class. There were seven first years and four second years. Ten men and one woman. The room next to the library in Bishop's House was overcrowded. Strung across the chimneypiece was a white board which shuddered every time Stephany applied to pen to it. On it she had written 'structuralism' for those who couldn't spell it and 'religion' to reassure those who felt that sociology didn't have anything to say in that area. This was the class which Aidan would normally have attended. Stephany didn't find any difficulty in having her husband in her class, any more than she had found it difficult to improve her New Testament Greek from him. But she suspected Aidan had reservations about sociology, despised, even, the foundations of her subject. He was a classicist. He had once said a close study of Thucydides was all that was necessary for you to acquire a thorough insight into the ways in which a society becomes corrupt. And that, he'd said with finality, is what priests need to know about.

As for the rest of the students, Stephany was beginning to wonder if this sort of teaching was the most effective way of skilling them for their tasks as spiritual leaders. It seemed to her that the course, apart from her own contribution, was a nineteenth-century one designed for young men who were already deeply imbued with linguistic and historical studies. Such a course would teach them *about* religion but not how to *be* religious.

'What do we mean by religious practices?' she asked.

The first years were silent in case they got it wrong.

No point in earning a reputation for being a moron before you had to, many of them felt.

'Prayer,' ventured Rita who had prudently borrowed a set of notes on Stephany's class from a previous second year.

'Right,' said Stephany. 'Religious practices are all those things which religious people do which non religious people do not do. Prayer and . . .' she urged them on.

'Worship.'

'Pilgrimage.'

'Feasting and fasting.'

'Meditating on Scripture.'

They'd caught on by now.

'Forming communities, churches.'

'How about hockey?' It was Trevor.

'Go on.'

'Well, I've got this team out at Cowley and me and Father Ron run it for a pack of lads that don't have jobs Monday afternoon.' He stopped. Had he missed the point? Was he being, as Rita would say, a bus driver again?

'You don't need to be religious to do that. Anyone can do it,' said one of his fellows.

'Anyone can but they don't,' Trevor defended himself.

'Do you play fair?' Stephany inquired.

Trevor was shocked. 'No point else.'

'Do they?'

'They're learning,' Trevor admitted.

'Anything Trevor does with unemployed lads they'll be able to learn from,' said Rita. 'He's a good example.'

Trevor was much moved by her loyalty. He'd got it right.

'Who sweeps a room as for thy laws,' said Isaiah suddenly. And felt happy. He'd got it right too.

'Right,' said Stephany. 'That's what makes religion different from life. We, you, offer not just words but examples. Preaching touches few. Scholarship accomplishes only a little. Nothing is more potent in human affairs than good example.' She thought of Duff and Dan. 'If the Church can't provide examples then it can't hope to irrigate society.'

In any proper learning context they'd leave it there. But they were scholars, supposedly. They had to pretend. The apparatus of essays and reading lists were there to confirm essentially simple truths. She thought about Dan again and felt the ache which his absence created in her. Dare she ring Tim Wade? Perhaps she'd try and get hold of Theodora over lunch and see what she felt.

The afternoon calm settled on the college. Through her open window Theodora could smell the nutty smell of autumn leaves rotting and, somewhere, being burnt. One or two students were dispersing from the refectory in the direction of the library or the small tussocky field which did duty as football or cricket pitch according to season. She caught sight of Trevor's green pullover disappearing under heavy leathers, after which he mounted his motorbike and roared off down the drive.

The events of the morning had left her without concentration. What am I doing? she asked herself. Waiting. Waiting for Richeldis Duff's chronology of the day her husband died. But waiting isn't an action, it's a state, and one which precludes anything being achieved. She looked at her stacked notes with regret. If there was no help for it, she must discover who had had a hand in Conrad Duff's death. Who, therefore, did she need to check on?

A list-maker by nature and training, she looked round for paper. The only thing available was her notebook on Esther Newcome. She turned to the back and ruled out three columns: 1. Who was *present* either on site or actually in the room on the day he died? As she wrote she realised she wasn't even sure of the date of Duff's death. 2. Who would have had a *motive* for wanting him dead? 3. Who had the *means* to kill him?

The third column was the easiest to fill. If it wasn't suicide, and for the moment she was ruling that out as psychologically improbable, Duff's death had come about because he'd lacked his medication. It was death by deprivation rather than by active cause; it was deprivation of life rather than a perpetration of death. Theodora wondered if there was a special term in law or moral philosophy to describe this. She could think only of Clough's line about not officiously striving to keep alive. But, given that cause, would it not widen the number of suspects with motivation? Surely there would be more people in the world, in the world of Gracemount, able to settle with their consciences by depriving Duff of the means of life rather than by supplying the means of death. But then perhaps churchmen with finicky consciences didn't get involved in such moves in the first place.

Under the first heading she could place Richeldis, Crispin, Brink, Dan, Mrs Gainley. Then she added, where were the Spins? Then, under the second heading, she put Richeldis, Crispin and anyone who might appear in what Richeldis had called the 'part two' material which Duff intended using for his Crockford preface. Theodora sat up. Where would that material be? Wasn't Brink supposed to be Duff's executor? Would he know? Had he perhaps found that material? And at what point? Before or after Duff's death?

Stephany's tap at the door was a relief. 'Richeldis gave me this just now,' she said and put down a brown envelope on Theodora's table, 'And Theo,' she pressed on, 'would you do me a favour?'

Theodora's ungenerous thought was, not another person wanting me to undertake impossible tasks. Why don't I just go back to my parish and forget all this?

'Yes,' she said, 'of course. What can I do?'

'You know Dan's been off colour since Conrad's death and I guess that's why he went off so suddenly on Saturday night to Tim Wade's. Well, he hasn't phoned or anything and I just thought . . .'

'Yes,' said Theodora, 'I'll go.'

'I hoped you would. I knew you would. I mean, you've known Dan longer than me. If I go it'll look as though I'm pursuing him. I don't want to pressure him at all.' She stopped. She looked near to tears.

It would have been easy for Theodora to say, it'll be all right, it's nothing to worry about. Parish experience had taught her not to say such things. They were never true. She'd go and see what Aidan and Wade were up to and then what she could do to help.

'Where shall I find Tim Wade?'

'Oh, he's quite grand. He's got a studentship at Christ Church and posh rooms in Peckwater.'

'Do you want to come along? Sit in the car?'

'Yes, I do, of course, but I can't leave Jamie and Henry.'

True nobility would have said, bring them too. But, Theodora felt, there are limits.

As she drove she thought, I move from cliché to cliché. Autumn everywhere and now Oxford, a city I least in the world want to see. It was deeply bound up with memories of her own youth and undergraduate life and of her father whose last living before his untimely death had been in north Oxford. It seemed to her that Oxford was a place which lived in memory more than in life. It was almost impossible to see it clearly. She felt that when she reached the stage of being able to visit Oxford without the disabling set of emotions she always experienced, then she would be truly grown up. She would have learned whatever it was necessary for her to have learned.

And then there was Aidan. He'd been such a golden boy, though dark-haired, in his undergraduate days. He'd been so easy, so at ease. 'A smooth runner', someone had said. He'd been dining with All Souls fellows before the end of his first year. He never appeared to work. Later Theodora had been surprised and amused to find that Aidan rose at five in order to do four hours' reading before most men's work began. He preferred to keep effort hidden. What else had Aidan kept hidden from the world, from his wife?

Peckwater was full of Japanese, each with at least two cameras slung round them like harnesses. Her height made her feel as though she were stepping, Gulliver-like, over their small forms. She paused to take in the never to be ignored beauty of the quadrangle. The House had been Newcome's college where, she remembered, he had felt himself, a pious youth, out of sympathy with the worldliness of the cathedral clergy. She wondered which had been his rooms.

Tim Wade's staircase was at the Canterbury Gate end. The outer door was open but the inner one closed. There was no answer to her knock. Of course, she should have rung first. But some sense of Wade's dislike of her formed at their first meeting had held her back. If she'd said she was coming and given the reason, he might have ducked out. She knocked again. Listening, she heard the sound of someone cautiously clearing a throat. She knocked again. Come on, Tim. Human hearts are in your hand.

The door was opened suddenly by Aidan. He stepped back. Was he surprised, embarrassed, guilty? Theodora wondered.

'Stephany sent you?'

'Not exactly sent. She's naturally worried.'

Aidan gestured her into Tim's room. Of Tim himself there was no sign. The remains of a lunch of bread and cheese and a half of bitter stood on the desk. Everywhere else there were books, neatly piled but leaving little space for any other sort of activity but reading. Through the second of the two windows opening on to the quad Theodora could see the stumpy yellow stone spire of the cathedral.

Theodora scrutinised Aidan to see what she would need to say. Never a fat man, he was thinner than she remembered him a couple of days ago. She noticed that his black hair was beginning to show grey round the ears and at its ends. He was wearing a none too clean fawn pullover and grey chinos. He's running down, she thought, annoyed at herself for caring, at him for being so. Hell's teeth, Aidan and Stephany were highly educated adults with all the privileges that confers; each, too, had a strong religious commitment. What more was necessary for successful living, for God's sake?

'Aidan, what is all this?' She was resolved not to let him off the hook.

'All what?' He could not, using those words, sound other than childish.

'Leaving your wife and children without giving them a reason. Mooning about like a teenager, skipping classes. What sort of an example do you suppose you're setting for people less gifted, less blessed than you?'

'You sound like a schoolteacher.'

'No more honourable profession, after priest.'

'Look, Theo . . .' He stopped. There was a sound of feet ascending the staircase. A moment later Timothy Wade entered. Aidan looked relieved and expectant. Wade stared at both of them, then looking at Theodora he said, 'Dan's not well.'

'It's not certain, Tim.'

'What's not certain?' But Theodora knew the answer. Why had she not guessed? All that refraining from contact with his wife and children could point only to one sickness, the sickness of our time, she thought.

'Look,' Wade leaned urgently towards Theodora. 'He can't come home yet. He's better off here. You're all better off if he doesn't come home just yet.'

'Until it's certain,' Aidan contributed.

Theodora wondered what it was like to live so immediately under the shadow of death. To know, to be able to predict the hour rather than simply holding it at a distance in a liturgical formula 'now and at the hour of our death'. She thought then how much she had liked, did like, Aidan. Had she not relished, amid a set of extrovert and contending egos, his under-statedness, his competence in whatever he took up, his generosity which had showed itself in original kindnesses. She looked at his face and hands. They seemed to her now shrivelled, like his spirit. She would not add to his difficulties but nevertheless she needed to question him out of Wade's presence.

'All right,' she answered Wade. 'I quite understand.' She turned to Aidan. 'Dan, would you walk me round the quad? I've got to be able to give Stephany something.'

It looked for a moment as though Wade would object but Aidan rose and opened the door for her. 'Ten minutes,' he said to Wade as though Wade were his keeper.

As they clattered down the stairs, Theodora made her plans. There was nothing she could do for Aidan, not a great deal she could do for Stephany but she intended to put a stop to whatever was, had been, going on at Gracemount. What a set of incompetents they all were. It was almost as though they had a death wish. Where Richeldis's behaviour left her divided, resentful and therefore reluctant, Aidan's turpitude simply made her angry and therefore prepared to act.

They emerged into the crowd of Japanese and of one accord made for Canterbury Gate, Merton Lane and the Meadow.

'You've got to tell me all you can.' Theodora was incisive. She, everyone, had delayed too long. 'Then

I'll tell you what I know and we'll see what can be done.'

'Don't make a *list* of me.' Aidan's spirit returned for a moment. 'Where do I start?'

'Gracemount and Duff's influence there.'

'We came here, as you know, just after we had Jamie, four years ago.'

Hell's teeth, thought Theodora, driven by anxiety and impatience, the linear narrative, biography the clue to all explanation. Really, how very unsophisticated the elaborately educated were when their own little personal tragedies were concerned.

'It seemed providential,' Aidan was maundering on. 'Steph had just finished her doctorate. She was doing a part-time NSM curacy at St Mark's and really it was all getting a bit much for her with two young children. I'd been to ABM and they'd accepted me, so when the Gracemount job came up for Steph, we thought we were all set. I mean Steph has so much to offer, don't you think?'

Theodora considered the merits of sociology as an academic discipline and Stephany's straightforward, almost infant-like Christian faith. 'She has a rich mix of talents,' she agreed. Then she thought, that's patronising. 'She's a dear,' she said with her whole heart.

The wall of Corpus Fellows' garden ended and they turned into the Meadow under Merton wall. The toadflax struggled out from the limestone for one last flowering before winter, the valerian had already turned to brown seed pods. The Meadow's always empty, Theodora thought.

'Of course, I knew Conrad's reputation before I went.'

Which reputation would that be? Theodora wondered but left it to Aidan to make his own pace.

'He might have been a scholar, I suppose, if he'd gone on with his church history studies. But in the end he made for, well, I suppose one could only call it power. Forming contemporary opinion, is what he called it.'

Come on, thought Theodora, get to the point.

'I mean, you saw what he published, the occasional pieces.' Aidan seemed anxious for her approval. 'Some of it was quite brilliant.'

'But no sustained work, no great opus.'

'No. He preferred cultivating people. Two sorts, the established, nice and successful in politics, the media and the universities, and then young men who might be in those positions in due course.'

'No rough trade?'

'None. For Conrad you had to be well connected, good-looking and clever.'

'You fitted?'

Aidan smiled. 'I passed muster. I think he realised his time was passing and he couldn't choose any more. He hadn't, you see, reached the top of his particular tree and, besides that, the tree itself was beginning to rot. During his lifetime the Church had begun to fail as a worldly power. It must have felt like running very fast to keep where you were.'

'You're reconciled to that?'

'Oh yes. Aren't you? One wouldn't want a bandwagon. And the Church needs utterly to change the way it serves the world. All this ravening for power must finish. The Franciscan model is the only effective one for our age. We've simply got to offer alternatives to money and control.'

In that case, Theodora thought, why didn't you keep yourself unspotted from the world? However, she held her peace and as they came in sight of Magdalen tower he pressed on.

'Well, anyway, there we all were, circling round Conrad, jockeying for his favour. "Who's in, who's out?" type stuff.'

'Who's "we"?'

Aidan regarded the golden light on the tower for a moment or two. 'The river or the Botanical Garden?' he inquired.

'As you wish.'

'I find the garden calms the nerves.'

Your fault you've got nerves, Theodora thought grimly. 'Who's "we"?' she pressed him again. If Duff had been murdered, 'we' was important.

'Matthew, of course.'

'Brink?' She was startled that he should put him first.

'From way back when.'

'An old flame?'

Aidan nodded.

'And?'

'Spin.'

'Spin?'

'I *think*. But he may have been one that got away. Certainly they were scarcely on speaking terms towards the end. Then of course Tim.'

Why didn't I think of that? Theodora thought. The enigmatic Tim Wade. Where did he fit in?

'But you were current star?'

'He took a liking. And I was useful.'

'How?' She dreaded the answer.

'He'd started writing again. As you say, he had no magnum opus. He knew time was running out. If he was going to get the top prize, he had to have something substantial to his name. He called it his "message to the nation", *The Darkened Glass*. It was going to be a definitive review of the Church's role in the modern world. I suppose a bit like your man Newcome's *Cities of Men*.'

Not much like. Theodora kept her reservation to herself. So that was how Duff had sold the Crockford preface to Aidan, was it? She didn't know who to be angrier with, the corrupt old Conrad or the gullible Aidan. 'And your part was?'

'I helped with the research. My Greek's better than his, both for the early church sources and the Greek fathers.'

How clever of Conrad to get a bright young research assistant who doted on him to do his work for him, Theodora reflected. 'And when did this start?'

'As soon as we came. I started almost at once. The idea was that it should be finished this September. Only . . .'

'Only something went wrong.'

'Yes. For one thing Conrad wasn't well. The way we worked was, he'd prepare a draft of what he wanted to say and then I'd do the historical bits and work it up into something coherent to carry the argument. But the drafts got briefer and harder to do anything with and finally dried up altogether.'

'When?'

'The end of this summer term. June. He begged me to stay put over the long vac. Well, no problem really. We don't have anywhere else to live. We generally go

to my mother's place but she's getting on a bit for
having young children round the house so it wasn't
difficult to persuade Steph to stay on.'

'Then what?'

'The rest you know. We footled about a bit over July
and August. We hadn't done a great deal more by the
beginning of September and on the eighth he died.'

Well, at least I now know the day of his death,
Theodora thought and remembered the unopened
letter from Richeldis waiting for her at Gracemount.

'Duff's illness was?'

'Heart.'

'But he had AIDS too?'

'I fear so. I mean I think that's why he took his
life.'

'And that's your fear? I mean, your fear for yourself?'

'It's a possibility.'

'How did you discover?'

'Tim knew. He warned me.'

'And told you to go for a test.'

'Yes.'

'When?'

'A week ago.'

'How did Tim know?'

'I think he knew Conrad's doctor. It was something
he said.'

'Spender?'

'Yes.'

Mentally Theodora added Spender to the list of
people she might need to see. 'So on your theory Conrad
killed himself?'

Aidan nodded.

'How?'

'Threw away his medicine bottle, by the look of it. Certainly it wasn't in his pocket when I found him in the garden.'

'So what are you planning to do now?'

They had turned under the rusticated gate of the Botanical Garden and paused for a moment before entering.

'I've got to be sure. I don't want to alarm Stephany unnecessarily.'

A fine way to go about it, Theodora thought.

'But obviously it's easier if I'm away from them all for the time being. And, of course, I'll have to give up the priesthood whichever way it goes.'

With that, at least, Theodora concurred.

'So could you, do you think, possibly cope with Stephany, deal with things at that end until . . . ?'

'Until when?' It was terrible to see him so reduced as to be asking dishonourable favours.

'Until I know the result of the test. It's another three days.'

Theodora considered. Fallen idols should earn their favours, she reckoned. The question was, how much to reveal. They turned into the central walk towards the statuary at the end of the garden. 'I'll do what I can for you, if you'll help me.'

Aidan signified assent. Or maybe it was relief.

'Richeldis Duff agrees with you that Conrad's death was not a natural one.' She held up her hand to stop Aidan interrupting. 'Hang on a minute. Her story agrees with yours that the medication he was on for his heart was missing when he had his attack. It wasn't among his things. But she thinks someone purloined it and whoever did so was responsible for his death.'

Theodora thought that was quite sufficient for Aidan at the moment. No need to mention Mrs Gainley's contribution about the medicine bottle in Brink's in tray.

'Richeldis isn't reliable, you know.'

'She seemed sure about this. And what's more, she's going to make a fuss to the trustees about Conrad, about his death, if she can't find out who was responsible.'

'If she's right, I suppose it could be that brute of a son. Just the sort of joker's move he would make.'

Theodora could see that having resolved to give up his priestly intentions, Aidan was going to speak as he found.

'Richeldis doesn't think so. And to help her prove that he's not guilty of his father's murder, she's set me on.' Theodora wondered if she should tell Aidan about the Newcome papers and decided not to.

'How do you mean, "set you on"?'

'Asked me to find out who is guilty.'

Aidan chewed this over. 'Why should you? Why doesn't she go to the police?'

'She wants proof or at least evidence first. Before she makes a fuss.' She thought Aidan was going to ask, but why you? But he didn't. Perhaps in view of his own reliance on her he felt it was only natural that Richeldis should get her to do her investigation for her.

'So what do you want me to do?' Aidan asked.

'Go over that day, the day of Conrad's death. Tell me anything that you can remember which might help. In particular the movements of everyone on that day.'

'I'll have to think.'

'Of course.'

'I'll ring you tomorrow, about lunch time.' Aidan stroked the curve of the huge stone urn. He seemed relieved, cheerful almost. 'Where are you going now?'

'To the market,' Theodora answered, 'to calm my nerves.'

CHAPTER EIGHT

University Challenge

Half an hour before closing time on a Monday, Oxford's covered market was practically empty. To the well-remembered smell of meat, sawdust and roasting coffee was added the more recent aroma of curry. Theodora had in mind the purchase of a modest quarter of Earl Grey from Cardew's to supplement the Gracemount refectory's brew which tasted like concentrated washing-up water.

She saw Maria Locke Tremble before Maria Locke Tremble saw her but even so it was too late. Mrs Locke Tremble waved her up like an insistent traffic policeman. She was leaning over the cold counter in Davidson's, butcher and poulterers, best Oxfordshire game. The habits of provincial housewives in France remained undulled in Mrs Locke Tremble in spite of thirty years' residence in England. She was expertly pinching the breasts of the free-range chickens while the butcher watched and winced.

'How goes the quest?' Mrs Locke Tremble called across the shop. The butcher raised his eyes momentarily from Mrs Locke Tremble's depredations to gaze at Theodora, as it seemed, imploringly.

No time like the present for furthering it, Theodora thought. 'So very glad to have bumped into you,' she remarked briskly and untruthfully. 'One or two points I'd value your advice on.'

'One moment while I conclude my affairs,' Mrs Locke Tremble commanded, and, extracting her purse, she made the unwilling assistant verify the presence of liver and giblets before counting out the price in twenty-pence pieces.

'A good chicken can do me and Fifi for a week,' Mrs Locke Tremble remarked.

Theodora expressed admiration.

'I am en route for Blackwell's music department,' Mrs Locke Tremble went on, shaking the bird down into a capacious raffia bag. 'Would you care to accompany me?'

Mrs Locke Tremble was a short woman with a short stride. Theodora was a tall woman with a long one. The pavements between the market and the Broad are not wide enough to allow two people to walk side by side. The result was a jerky conversation.

'Have you,' Mrs Locke Tremble's voice rang out, 'established our young man's innocence? Have you apprehended the guilty one?'

Theodora was tempted to say she was neither the Hound of Heaven nor Maigret. 'I've managed to have a word with Richeldis,' she said cautiously, 'and she seems to feel she knows the cause of death.'

'Poison,' said Mrs Locke Tremble with drama.

'No. Absence of medicine.'

'The same thing.'

'Not quite.' Theodora would have liked to have debated with someone the difference between depriving of life and causing death. She gazed down the length of the Broad and thought of the number of lawyers and moral philosophers the street must have. The fronts of Trinity and Balliol, the back of Jesus, the end of Hertford, the beginning of Wadham. The place must be stuffed with people who had thought about this distinction. 'Never there when you need them,' she murmured to herself.

'*Pardon?*'

'I said, I need to establish a timetable for the day of Conrad's death. Also to try to find the motive. Can you help me with either of these?'

'The motive will not be difficult. So many people wanted to kill Conrad,' Mrs Locke Tremble shouted over the heads of two pedestrians who momentarily separated them on the narrow pavement.

'Such as?' Theodora's tone was quieter.

'The whole world abhorred him,' said Mrs Locke Tremble unhelpfully.

'We must be specific. How about Matthew Brink?'

'Him, I never liked.'

Theodora felt she might have predicted as much.

'He is pompous and sly.'

'How do you know him so well?'

'Am I not the organist of St Sylvester's parish church? Have I not heard him preach many a time? Nothing more reveals a man's character than his words from the pulpit.'

Theodora felt this at least was true.

'He stands in for Toby Spin during the latter's frequent absences.' Mrs Locke Tremble spotted a gap in the boiling traffic and loped across the Broad.

'Not enough to provide a motive for murder,' Theodora found herself shouting after her above the traffic. Mrs Locke Tremble's habit of public debate was catching.

'Then there is Spin himself.' Mrs Locke Tremble pronounced the 'i' long, which certainly made him sound sinister. 'There is a louche character.'

'Why?' Theodora was tiring of Mrs Locke Tremble's blanket condemnation of mankind.

'He has no children, he and his nurse wife. What are they doing with themselves?'

Theodora felt this was really most unfair. 'That's their concern,' she said breathlessly as they swung into Holywell.

'Well, he did not care for Warden Duff. He had failed to advance his, I mean Spin's, career.'

'How?'

'References were not forthcoming for Spin. He wanted a post in college as a master of music. Down there, I think.' Mrs Locke Tremble gestured with her bag full of chicken in the direction of New College. Theodora's mind boggled. Toby Spin as director of music of New College? Surely not.

'He was ambitious, that one, to experiment with the liturgy. But he is not as proficient at the organ as he thinks.'

'I hardly think of New College as an innovator in either music or liturgy.'

'That is what Warden Duff told him,' Mrs Locke Tremble said with satisfaction.

'How do you know?'

'Crispin heard the matter being debated.'

Theodora did not find it too difficult to imagine Crispin with his ear to a keyhole. 'What about Crispin himself? Are you sure he couldn't have taken his father's medication at the operative moment?'

'That good boy, *très doué*, has done nothing wrong. Of that I am convinced. On the day of the death of his father, after the unfortunate altercation, he came to me. I consoled him. We played a little on the chamber organ. Poulenc, I seem to remember. I gave him a little *déjeuner*. He departed some time after two o'clock. And returns, alas, to the scene of death.'

I can check all that, Theodora thought, against Richeldis's chronology. Blackwell's music department loomed ten yards ahead of them. Theodora had no intention of continuing this conversation at Mrs Locke Tremble's pitch inside its doors. 'So how about the other two, Aidan Prior and Tim Wade?'

'That will be your task to discover,' said Mrs Locke Tremble, swirling her basket through the glass door of the shop.

The brown envelope contained a single sheet of lined A4. It lay on Theodora's desk in the attic room waiting for her return. It was headed in melodramatic fashion, 'The Warden's Last Day, September 8th'. Under it was written a note in Richeldis's large round hand: 'I've put in as much as I can remember. It's up to you to cross check where there are doubts.' Underneath was the following list:

RD = Richeldis Duff; CD = Conrad Duff.
5.30 a.m.   RD up. Crispin already up.
7.15   CD up, out for walk. (He usually did

	this. It was the sole exercise of his day. I do not know where he went.)
8 a.m.	RD breakfast. Crispin looked in but did not breakfast.
8.15	CD breakfast.
9 a.m.	CD to his college study. Crispin went into garden with books to work (AL preparation). N.B. CD was wearing grey flannels and his linen jacket, in the inside pocket of which was his Atroxine.
9.30	Ellenor Spin called.
10.15	CD back from college study to his study in our apartment. I heard him open French doors on to garden.
10.25	RD to village for stamps and fish fingers.
11.45	RD returned from village. No sign of Crispin. Thelma Gainley brought papers from college and talked with Conrad by now seated in garden; left 12 noon.
12.30	Heard Crispin and Conrad conversing, quarrelling in garden.
1 a.m.	Luncheon à deux in dining room. Fish fingers, broccoli, apple charlotte, cheese and coffee. No Crispin.
1.45	RD washed up and went for lie-down with *The Times* crossword. DC went back to work in garden.
2.30	RD woken by kerfuffle in garden. Brink and Aidan Prior both there. They carried CD indoors to the study

	then upstairs to his bedroom. I looked in Conrad's pocket for his Atroxine but found none. I rang Maria Locke Tremble for Crispin. Then Brink rang for Dr Spender.
2.50	Crispin returned. Conrad died approx 3.15.
3.45	Dr Spender came and shook his head.

How banal our goings out and our comings in are, Theodora thought as she skimmed through this catalogue of domestic trivia. It was no more revealing than Esther Newcome's effusions to her sister on jaunts to the opera. It certainly was not, on the surface, any great help in discovering who killed the Warden if, indeed, he had been killed. Or, to put it another way, who removed the medicine from his jacket so that when he needed it, it wasn't there. Crispin's movements more or less tallied with what Maria Locke Tremble had said about a quarrel with his father and his visiting her. Presumably Richeldis knew enough of Crispin's habits to know where to telephone him when his father was taken ill.

Two questions needed to be asked. Firstly, what were Brink and Aidan doing visiting Duff at the time of his collapse? Had they a common errand? Aidan she could question directly when he phoned tomorrow. Brink she could probably make a start on at his supper party tonight. Secondly, there was the question of the suicide note. Where had it come from and when and by whom had it been placed in Duff's bedroom?

She had an hour to go before she needed to think

about getting herself to Brink's party. She could either go back to the Newcome notes or press on putting her thoughts in order. Or, of course, she could go and comfort Stephany. She had gone to the flat immediately on her return from Oxford. Stephany and the boys had been out. Theodora had been relieved. She felt she really could not face Stephany at this moment. It would inevitably mean lying or at the very least leaving things unsaid. She had left a note, the tone of which she had carefully calculated to avoid being either falsely hearty or too reassuring, saying that she had seen Aidan. He sent his love but could not at the moment face either his family or his academic work. He'd be in touch before the weekend. If Stephany concluded from this that he was about to have a breakdown, well, there wasn't anything much she could do about it.

Theodora pulled her Esther notebook towards her and flicked to the end to see how she was doing. In spite of Maria Locke Tremble's remarks about the number of Conrad's enemies, it was the column marked 'motive' which was going to cause the difficulty. Could she add under motive for Spin the quarrel over job references? Would this provide a motive for murder, if nothing more was required to bring about death than withholding medicine at the very moment it was needed? Surely only for a madman. And Richeldis's chronology did not reveal that he'd had any contact with Conrad on the day of his death. On the other hand, Mrs Spin had been at the house earlier in the day. Then there was the question of Crispin. What had he been quarrelling with his father about? He certainly had motive; there was a lifetime's animosity between father and son. Could he have removed his father's medicine?

More difficult to face was the question of Aidan. She looked again at the motive column. He, if what he had revealed this afternoon was right, had a motive. He could have wished simply to stop Duff going on as he had. He might, too, have felt guilt at his own conduct. She remembered Aidan's tone when they were eating together on the evening of her arrival, Saturday night. 'He shouldn't have died,' he'd said. She'd felt at the time there had been too much emotion in his utterance. What was the nature of that emotion? Was it remorse? Had Dan, was Dan capable of taking another man's life? Was someone she'd known, admired and trusted capable of such an act?

But what about Richeldis herself and her own bona fides? She had the motive all right; twenty years of misery with Conrad had given her that. She had certainly had the opportunity. But why then, if she really did want Conrad dead, did she want to stir things up? She had said, and Maria Locke Tremble had backed this, that she wished to free Crispin of his feeling of guilt. But what if Crispin had indeed killed his father, not merely by quarrelling with him and precipitating his attack but by stealing his medication and making sure he did not recover from it?

Theodora tried to bring the character of Conrad Duff into focus. It wasn't, after all, such an uncommon type either in academic or ecclesiastical life. Dons who gathered courts of young men round them were often regarded as merely extending the duties of teaching into those of hospitality and friendship. Often no harm and much good came from such associations. Theodora could think of several distinguished men who had been about in her own time at university for whom the young men so recruited had nothing but admiration. The tastes of youth had been cultivated and refined. Older men had, in turn, been refreshed by the company of youth, their own sympathies extended. Surely nothing but good could come from that.

In the Church, too, curates were taught and bishops gathered their young hopefuls as chaplains and dining companions. If such friendships went on over the years, it was really nothing more than a network of *beneficia* and *officia* which led to jobs being filled, talents found scope in spheres which benefited society – which had, after all, to be run by someone. Women, she reflected, having lower places in the public scheme of things, were less exposed both to the opportunities and temptations.

Only occasionally, it went wrong. Occasionally, the retinues became arenas for manipulation or the gratification of the wish to dominate. What then? Then, thought Theodora grimly, you had families and proper duties neglected. Then, you had passions wrongly channelled. Then, you had a finale of murder.

The smell of lighter fuel only slightly tinctured with sausage met Theodora as she made her way towards Matthew Brink's quarters on the other side of the Bishop's House from the Warden's apartments. Her heart sank. She was hungry after the labours and excitements of the day. The smell did not bode well for its satisfaction. She distrusted Brink as an organiser in worldly matters.

Sure enough, at the far end of the terrace a flimsy

looking and rather small barbecue had been set up. A group of guests was clustered around it to urge it on. Theodora could see the Spins, Thelma Gainley and several of what must be students. She was reminded of her own tutor's insolent remark that she could never tell one undergraduate from another, they all looked the same. But as she got older Theodora recognised what she meant. They lacked histories to differentiate them and their present experiences and preoccupations were all identical.

'Now isn't this fun?' Mrs Spin's brogue caught her ear. 'Lovely grub.'

Theodora looked at her in amazement. Matthew Brink, pink and sweating where he was not besmirched with charcoal, looked up with relief. 'Ah, Miss Braithwaite, how very nice to see you. I wonder, are you by any chance an expert in these contraptions?'

Theodora saw that if they were to get any supper, she had better be. She rolled up the sleeves of her aunt's dress and took the bellows from Brink's unresisting hand. Relief could be read on all faces.

Once assured of food in the not too distant future, the senior members swung into party mode. Brink took on Thelma, Spin made himself agreeable to the students. Mrs Spin showed a disposition to hover round Theodora so Theodora made her work turning the meat.

'Did you manage to get a break over the summer?' Theodora asked guilelessly.

'Well, no, we did not. Normally we go to my sister's little cottage in County Antrim. But this year they were all having the measels. So we thought it best not to venture. Did you get a break yourself, Theo?'

Mrs Spin inquired with what Theodora thought was too much warmth.

'This is my break,' she answered bleakly. 'So you were around the day the Warden died. That must have been a great comfort to everyone.' She was aware she was mimicking Mrs Spin's diction and only hoped she hadn't also copied her accent which was catching.

Mrs Spin didn't seem to notice anything. 'I remember the day,' she said, 'as though it was yesterday. Toby had walked up to see Conrad, as it happened.'

'When would that have been?'

'Oh, about threeish. It's a pity he didn't get up there a bit sooner. He might have been able to do something.'

'And could he?'

'Well, I always think it helps to have a minister when there's a death in a family. Not,' she added, 'that they were lacking priests. What with Dan and Matthew with him when he went, the poor soul. And then of course Wade came along after it was all over. Some people have that sort of timing, don't you find? They miss by a hair's breadth the great events of life.' Mrs Spin was struck by the profundity of her thought.

'Wade?'

'To be sure. Toby, didn't you say Tim Wade was at Conrad's the day he died?'

Toby Spin had drifted up for his share of the goodies. Theodora handed him a well-cooked slice of steak wrapped in pita bread and loaded with salad. He looked cheered at this, emptied his glass and applied himself to eating.

'Yep. Poor old bloke. Talk about dying in peace. I must say the whole thing was operatic.' Toby assimilated the events to his own genre. 'I was just chorus. By the time I got there he was dead but Matt told me all about it. Conrad had had his fit or whatever in the garden. When Brink and Dan got there they arsed about trying to revive him when obviously they should have been ringing for an ambulance. Then Richeldis came on the scene. She wouldn't do anything until Crispin arrived.'

'Where was he?'

'With our organist, Mrs Locke Tremble. You won't know her. She's a tremendous character. Rather above our heads musically. But she's taken a shine to young Crispin and gives him a bit of free tuition when either of them has a mind for it.'

'And he came up.'

'Yes. He was there to witness the end.'

'Spender was called only after Crispin appeared.'

'I suppose that's right.'

'Brink kept saying "He's got his Atroxine, hasn't he?" and Richeldis said he had.'

'And had he?'

'There was a bottle beside his bed.'

'When? I mean I thought he was supposed to keep it on him in his suit. Did anyone take it from his suit and put it beside the bed?'

'No. I don't think so. Anyway it was there when I got there.'

'And when did Wade arrive?'

'When Conrad was dead. I saw him as I left. I mean I felt there wasn't anything more I could do. I felt a bit in the way actually. And neither Richeldis nor Crispin wanted comforting. Actually Matt was the one in tears. After all, I wasn't close to Conrad Duff. So I went downstairs and Wade and Spender were coming through the door as I left.'

'Dr Spender's a fine man,' said Mrs Spin. 'He was an old buddy of Tim Wade's. Were they not at the university together, Toby?'

'No,' said Toby, 'no, that was Spender's father. But the son's taken on the father's mantle. All part of the network all right.' It struck Theodora that Toby was a bit drunk.

'How's the research going?' Matthew Brink took his pita and sausage in salad and attacked it with relish. 'The food's really turned out much better than I'd hoped,' he said.

Theodora reckoned it had too. She also reckoned she'd done her bit. She accepted her wine from Brink and took the last and best done of the steak by way of reward and prepared to pursue her own line with Brink. 'I haven't made as much progress as I'd hoped,' she admitted.

'People's lives,' he said expansively, 'such murky fields.'

Theodora took the bull by the horns. 'Will you be writing a life of Conrad Duff?'

'Well, I am his executor, his literary executor.' There was pride there. Did Brink think he'd won out? He'd been chosen from amongst them all. The wish to boast fought with discretion. 'I think Conrad's last work should consolidate his reputation. I've come across some interesting notes amongst his papers. Really first-rate stuff.'

'You mean the material Aiden drafted for *The Darkened Glass*?'

Brink digested this unwelcome bit of intelligence.

She'd got him. He didn't know about Aidan doing the work. He was thrown. 'Well, these things are rather Buggins' turn, aren't they? We all have to lend a hand with the chores in research.'

It sounded lame. Theodora saw no reason not to put the boot in. 'Still, a gentleman always acknowledges his sources.'

'Oh quite.' Brink took refuge in vagueness. Theodora watched him withdraw his attention from her. That would be how he coped with unpleasant difficulties, she judged.

She thought it worthwhile risking a final shot. *The Darkened Glass* was one thing, the Crockford preface quite another. Surely he must have known about it, being as he was, so close to Conrad. 'And the Crockford preface, too, is hardly an ordinary chore, is it?' Theodora's tone was friendly, equals and colleagues. Really, she was amazed at the man's patronage. Did he suppose that she did not know the worth of one of the most highly sought opportunities in the Anglican Church? She smiled sweetly at Brink munching the remains of the meat he had not the common wit to be able to cook. 'Not quite a chore, would you say? It has been known to challenge the credibility of archbishops in its time.'

CHAPTER NINE

Heroes and Heroines

'Could you ask your mother if she'd spare me a moment round about twelve thirty?' Theodora looked Crispin up and down. He was as skimpily dressed as always, in trainers, shorts and a singlet. Only today it looked to Theodora as though he was wearing lipstick and eyeliner as well. She did hope this had to do with his theatrical aspirations.

'Ma's not in,' said the boy, practised in disobliging.

'Perhaps you could ask her when she does come in.' Theodora swung her briefcase up the stairs to Newcome's room. She knew she wasn't handling Crispin well. He set her teeth on edge. She consoled herself that he had a friend in Mrs Locke Tremble.

The Newcome papers lay as she had left them arranged on the desk. There was a pile of letters which Theodora thought of as the domestic trivia, letters from Esther to her sister, perhaps returned to Newcome after her death. In addition there were the three shiny black-covered volumes of Newcome's diaries for 1879. Today, this very morning, she would make her way swiftly through all three and begin to index the material and fill in the chronology of the much longed for pre-publication year. She knew the danger was that she would become so immersed in what she was reading that she'd skimp on the recording and annotating. She was flooded by that immense pleasure that had been hers throughout her youth, a whole morning with nothing to do but read, a pleasure beyond telling. She pulled the first of the black diaries towards her and opened at the first entry, January 7th, 1879, and began to read.

It was better, far better than she had hoped. The handwriting was clear, well-formed copperplate, rather larger than she'd expected. Thomas Henry had apparently reversed the usual order of the scholar's day. He'd given the morning over to domestic matters and the afternoon to reading and the composition of his great work. So most entries provided an insight into the actions of a man running a small estate, teaching, as far as she could determine, a group of three young men reading for Anglican orders, and, at the same time, listing his reading and expanding his thinking for what was to be a monument of Anglican scholarship, the final portions of *Cities of Men*.

It was a portrait of a life both well and agreeably spent. Perhaps the late nineteenth century was the last time it had been possible to do this without guilt for the leisure and privilege which made it possible. There were extracts with notations from Ruskin, Pugin and William Morris side by side with quotations from the Fathers, particularly Clement of Alexandria. The effect was to show a mind at the height of its powers synthesising the best of modern and ancient thinking to provide a new vision. She saw, as never before, that his strength was in weaving the insights of individuals and their private spiritual practices into a set of public structures which could benefit the whole of society. She felt nothing but gratitude that she'd been allowed this experience. She read on steadily, immersing herself in the rhythm of Newcome's life.

The entries continued being written every two or three days until the tenth of March. After which there was a gap of almost three weeks. Theodora paused to consider why this might be. Might there, she wondered, be anything in the letters of Esther to her sister to account for it? Had Thomas Henry been sick or had he travelled abroad? She began to turn over the thicker paper of the letters. They were not in date order but just as she was about to give up and return to the diaries, she came across one dated Gracemount, March 10th, 1879. The handwriting was rushed, in places almost scrawled; there were smudges which seemed contemporary with the composition.

My beloved Emily, I write, as you see, in haste. Etty has at last left us. I cannot say with what relief I watched the train depart. Thus ends the period of my life I would least wish to live again. I know that you, my dearest sister, can be my only confidante in this matter since in you alone have I entire trust as to your discretion. Now that all is at last, as I pray and expect, concluded, I can confess that in my suffering I feel as though I have gained the wisdom of a hundred years within the space of a month. I know that men and women feel differently in these matters and that what is of first importance to women appears but trivial to men. But in the great scheme of things I cannot help but believe that our perceptions and affections will in the end be judged to be at the higher level. However, when it came to the dénouement, I confess that Thomas has such a streak of ingenuousness in him that he would not if he could hide the truth of his feelings from me. This is not the first time but I pray with my whole heart that it will be the last. I am resolved to take upon myself the work of amanuensis in the future to obviate all temptation. Once the daily contact is removed and temptation gone, then I am sure I can restore all that at present I feel trembling about me. What he writes I have long been familiar with, how he writes it will now become my peculiar task. And in this way we can keep to the straight path of virtue. My first concern shall be that in spite of all his anxieties and scruples, the work shall be finished and the world shall profit from his mature *wisdom nor my world be destroyed by what I am sure can be only a temporary infatuation. I can no more. But* you *shall know all in due time, my dearest sister. Your ever loving Esther.*

Theodora put the letter down beside the last diary entry for March tenth. Feverishly she began to look through the letters. Esther had written to her sister weekly. The next was dated March 17th, Sunday. Yes, there was more, as Esther had promised.

It is settled. We do not speak of Henrietta Cold-
harbour and I mean that we never shall. I trust
Thomas will in time put her out of his thoughts
even as she is out of our household. We have a
new modus operandi. In the morning Thomas
reads and I attend to my household duties. But
after luncheon, I change my 'role' and become,
as it were, an underlabourer. Though I have to
say, dear Emma, an underlabourer with all sorts
of privileges. As we advance down the path of
scholarship, I glean so much from his teeming
mind and yet Thomas is kind enough to say he
does not disdain the intuitions of the frailer sex.
All that I learned from being dear Papa's help-
meet, how many years ago that seems! I now put
to good use to be an aid to him whom in the world
I most revere.

Theodora allowed the letter to fall from her fingers
and marvelled at the low self-esteem of women. But
then she caught herself up. Had she not just now
thought how much a privilege it was to watch the
formation of the thought of her hero in his diaries?
Was that not what Esther, too, had thought? The
question she must pursue as a biographer was, how
much had Esther contributed to the thinking? Would
that be revealed in the diaries? And if Esther were as
strong intellectually as she had proved to be morally
and emotionally, should that not mean a very different
biography from the one she had originally projected?

What had she told Wade when he'd asked her, how
do you know in biography whether something is true?
What would convince you? Well, what had she found?

Esther talked of Thomas's 'infatuation', and 'not the
first time', so the picture of Newcome had to change.
Just as her picture of Esther had grown and modified.
Neither of them was what she had originally thought.
For a moment Theodora felt all the despair of a
deceived lover. He's failed me. Then she thought, but
how frightfully interesting. If *he* turns out more
ordinary than she had supposed, *she* is surely more
remarkable. So remarkable that it seemed unlikely
that she could continue her husband's biography in
quite the form she'd envisaged. She realised how much
she'd planned the episodes, set the tone to present
Newcome in heroic mode. She'd have to change all
that now.

Isaiah Ngaio placed his notes from four lectures in
order. He was not happy with them. His memory was
excellent, his culture not far removed from one which
was entirely oral. He had at home friends who had
converted to Islam who expected to know the Koran
by heart. And he himself knew long passages of
Scripture verbatim. But here in his classes he was
being told things which were not in themselves script-
ural, which were comments on, interpretations of it,
were in fact abstract and man made, not God made.
He had heard the words 'analytical' and 'critical' a great
deal and he wondered what they meant. He had the
phrase 'on the one hand and on the other'; he had
heard 'some scholars argue but others think'. But
surely the Truth was one and authenticated itself? It
was of God. There could be no question of divergent
views clamouring against each other like badly trained
children.

He had been set an essay on the sources of St
Matthew. Surely St Matthew had heard the words of
the Saviour, remembered them, recorded them and
sent them out into the world to save souls. But this
had not been the view expounded by the Reverend
Matthew Brink in this morning's class. Brink had
spoken of oral tradition as though this were unreliable,
he had spoken of the editors of oral material as though
they were necessarily liars. Isaiah was deeply disturbed.

When he had consulted with his friends, Trevor and
Rita, Trevor had said, 'I just copy bits out of the
textbooks, actually.' And Rita had said, 'Well, there
are always two sides to every question, aren't there?'
Isaiah wished to do well. He was aware that his stay
in England at Gracemount was costing his community,
by their standards, a great deal of money. He wished
to be a credit to it, to his Bishop and the Church in
Umundi, but it was beginning to look as though this
might be a harder task than he had at first envisaged.
He wondered if perhaps the excellent Miss Braithwaite
might be able to enlighten him. She, after all, knew
something of his culture; had she not greeted him in
exemplary fashion on their first meeting? He would
seek her out.

It was the moment of calm after lunch. There was
no one about. He padded along the corridor from his
own attic to Theodora's at the other end and tapped
on her door. There was no answer. Cautiously, respect-
fully, he opened the door and put his head round.
Squatting in the corner by the fireplace was Crispin
Duff. He had an iron lever in his hand with which he
appeared to be attacking the chimneypiece. Isaiah

gazed at Crispin. Crispin stared back at Isaiah.

'Get out,' said Crispin.

In any language that Isaiah knew this was not a possible way to greet guests. 'Are you here by Miss Braithwaite's invitation?' he inquired.

Crispin rose to his feet brushing dust and cinders from his singlet. 'Are you?'

'I seek her.'

'Well, I don't,' said Crispin and with that he took a last look at the chimney and, diving under Isaiah's arm, made for the staircase. In bafflement, Isaiah returned to his own room to pen a note to Theodora requesting the pleasure of a word or two if she had a moment to spare.

The doctor's surgery smelt of formaldehyde and disinfectant. Not so unlike a vet's, Theodora thought. She wondered what they needed to disinfect and what preserve that these two substances should be on the air. The nurse at the reception desk flanked by two computer screens had barked, 'Name?' Then, as the screen flickered, 'You haven't an appointment. You aren't Dr Spender's patient.'

'No. I rang earlier, about one thirty. I explained.'

'I wasn't on then. I don't come in till two.' The clock behind her said three forty-five.

'I spoke directly to Dr Spender. It's a private matter.'

'All our consultations are entirely confidential,' said the nurse as though her chastity had been impugned.

'Yes. Yes,' Theodora soothed. 'Dr Spender was kind enough to say he could give me five minutes after his last appointment at four. It's a family matter,' she unwisely added.

The nurse swept her with a glance and resorted to the intercom. She barked into it for a moment. There was a high-pitched yelp back from it. Apparently this wasn't a satisfactory response. The nurse-receptionist alias warder struck it viciously with her fist. It cackled belligerently to itself. Theodora knew just how it felt. The woman resorted to going to the back of the office, flinging open a hatch and consulting the oracle direct.

So much for the caring professions, Theodora thought, as she settled down to wait. Thank Heaven I'm not sick. The minimalist tubular steel and canvas chairs were designed to keep the sickly upright and in their place. On the low table in the middle of the room was a greyish plant of indeterminate breed not in good health. The human beings, none of them at their peak, hugged the wall, holding on to the chairs for safety's sake. At intervals the warder barked a name and one of these relinquished the canvas to totter to the door beside the reception desk.

'Cards?' growled the nurse. Patients would start guiltily and fumble them from her dismissive hand. Really, Theodora thought, she'd known veterinary surgeries run on more humane lines. At a quarter past four and with obvious reluctance, Theodora's name was called.

Dr Neville Spender, though for the most part bald, looked about twelve and a half. He was slumped in his chair as though in the last stages of exhaustion. When he took Theodora's measure, some atavistic memory of manners other than those to which he habitually worked caused him to half rise. But fatigue overcame him and he fell back before the action was fully achieved.

'Mrs Battenburg,' he said, 'what can I do for you?'
He looked in vain for his notes.

'Theodora Braithwaite. I rang earlier.'

Memory returned. 'Yes, yes, so you did,' he said
without conviction.

Theodora took from her briefcase the notes she had
made from her conversation with Richeldis that morning, supplemented by her lunchtime phone call from
Aidan. After checking the stories of the one against
the other, she reckoned she had just enough information. Someone was lying, all she had to do was to get
Dr Spender to show her who.

'It's very good of you to see me, Dr Spender.'
Theodora smiled confidently at him. Dr Spender looked
nervous. 'Canon Duff was, I believe, your patient.'

Theodora's manner was that of a competent QC.
Dr Spender had unhappy memories of QCs. There had
been a case which had gone against him during his
intern year at the Radcliffe. He did not want, he could
not afford, a repetition of anything like that. He put
himself on guard. 'If you've come here to discuss one
of my patients, I'm afraid I can't help you. Patient
confidentiality.'

Theodora smiled kindly at him. 'I'm acting,' she went
on in best official manner, 'on behalf of his widow, Mrs
Richeldis Duff, his son, Mr Crispin Duff, and of course,'
she touched her collar, 'the Church authorities of the
Oxford Diocese.' She'd just have to trust that the word
'Diocese' was as much a mystery to Dr Spender as it
was to most of the rest of the world, let alone the ways
in which he might check up on that statement.

Dr Spender jacked himself up a notch in his chair.
'I'm sure you're aware that Canon Duff was a very

distinguished, a very senior member of the Church,'
Theodora went on. Dr Spender knew no such thing.
He nodded sagely. 'The view of the authorities, supported by Mrs Duff, is that there should have been a
post mortem and an inquest following the death of
Canon Duff on,' Theodora pretended to consult her
notes, 'September the eighth this year. Our advice to
her is that she should approach the police and get the
coroner to act. An exhumation order.'

Spender became fully vertical. He remembered only
too well just what that had meant last time. Keep your
head, Neville, he told himself, staring with distaste
at this tall, composed bloody woman in her clerical
silly collar. 'On what ground would you, the Church,
the family,' he swallowed, 'the police want to exhume?'

'You did sign the death certificate, I believe?'

'There were no grounds not to. Conrad Duff had a
heart condition.'

'Which was controlled by the drug Atroxine, I
believe.'

Dr Spender nodded. What was the woman getting
at?

'How did you prescribe the Atroxine capsules for
Canon Duff? I mean at what intervals, how many and
on what occasion?' Dan had given Theodora the information on this one.

Dr Spender looked round his desk. 'I'll have to get
the records. My nurse . . .' he said, aware that his
answer did not engender confidence.

Theodora waited while Dr Spender opened his hatch
and murmured obsequiously to the other side. After
some time the notes were thrown through the hatch,
a bit like fish into the seal pond at the zoo. Dr Spender

fell on them with relief. 'He was prescribed as needed. He only needed to take Atroxine if he felt an attack coming on, palpitations, breathlessness, etcetera.'

'When did he last have a prescription?'

'August tenth.'

'How?'

'I pass his house, the college, on my way to surgery. I dropped in the new prescription.'

'And before that?'

Dr Spender looked again. 'July.'

'So he'd taken the July ones by the time he died. Had he?'

'What do you mean?'

'He was to take them when he had an attack. Right?'

'Right.'

'And if he had an attack you'd presumably want to see him. To check up?'

Spender nodded slowly. He could see only too clearly where this was leading.

'And did you check up after you'd prescribed in August?'

'Well, actually, no. As you say, he was a priest. One naturally trusted his word.'

'So he said he wanted more Atroxine capsules but you didn't check on whether he'd used up the previously prescribed ones.'

'Why should he say he wanted more Atroxine tablets if he didn't need them?'

'How did you learn that he wanted them? I mean, who told you?'

Dr Spender looked at his notes. 'There was a phone call from his house, his wife . . .' he said helplessly.

'What would happen, Dr Spender, if someone took

a double dose of Atroxiné?' Theodora leaned slightly forward to invade Spender's space.

Spender remained silent.

'They'd die, wouldn't they?' Theodora said quietly.

He couldn't deny it.

'My information is that at the time of his death, Canon Duff had ten capsules of Atroxine to hand. But the bottle beside his bed was empty.' She hoped she could trust Dan on this point. She hoped she could trust Dan's observation. She hoped he was right when he said Richeldis was lying about the absence of the bottle or bottles. Dan had been convincing. Theodora had put her money on Dan and if he was wrong she'd be lost. She studied Dr Spender's face. He was sweating slightly. She reckoned Dan might be right.

'There certainly was a bottle of Atroxine on the table beside Canon Duff's bed when I got to him,' he admitted.

'Empty or full?'

Dr Spender thought of the inquest, the exhumation order. They'd be able to tell if they dug him up. There was unfortunately no way out but the truth. 'Empty,' he said at last.

As she came out of his room, Theodora looked round the surgery, at the miserable chairs, the dying plant and the angry nurse beating the hell out of her computer. 'Good afternoon,' she said cordially to them all.

Henry put the last strut in place in his Meccano palace and tightened the bolt. Then he sat back on his heels to survey his work. He saw that it was good.

'Where's Daddy?' Jamie asked for the umpteenth time.

'Staying with Uncle Tim.' Henry was patient.

'Don't know Uncle Tim,' Jamie complained.

'I don't know him very well either. I've seen him with Daddy. He lives in Oxford.'

'Where's Oxford?' Jamie knew perfectly well where Oxford was but he needed to keep talking to reassure himself.

'Twelve miles down the road south-west.' Henry was learning to orientate himself at school. It was called 'Humanities' or, by the older members of staff, 'Geography'. He was looking forward to going back to school next week to do some more Humanities. If anyone had asked him, he'd have had to say it was all getting a bit boring at home. He'd heard his mother use the word 'stressed' and he wondered if that was what things were getting round here. When people said the word, he imagined a piece of elastic being stretched and stretched until it became nothing. Perhaps if people kept on bickering and evading *he'd* become nothing. He started to think what it would be like to be nothing.

'Where's Mummy?' Jamie changed tack.

'She's only just across in the library. She said she'd be back in twenty minutes.' The boys were not usually left alone but without Aidan, Stephany could hardly carry out her duties unless she occasionally left them. She did so in quick dashes consumed with guilt and praying that nothing untoward would befall them. She longed for the end of half-term and for Dan's return.

'Will she be very long?'

'Look, let's play computers,' Henry said. 'I'll teach you how to use it properly.' He was not too hopeful about this but felt it was worth a try. He'd done very well in his SATs last term, he'd heard his mother say, and part of that had been getting things into and (rather harder) out of computers. So he was game for a try.

'What do we do first?' Henry inquired in best didactic manner.

'Boot the system,' said Jamie joyfully. He loved the words.

'Right. Boot it then.'

Jamie crawled under the table and switched on the electrics. The ancient Amstrad cleared its throat, hummed and hawed a bit and flickered into life. The two young Cortezes gazed at the screen together.

'What's most fun,' Henry said, 'is to put something in and see where we land up.'

Henry looked through the box of disks. They said things like 'Early Church History Two' or 'Eschatology One'. Henry knew these weren't exciting. They had no pictures of buildings in any of them.

'It'll be better when Daddy gets a proper computer, one you can play games on and learn things from.' There had been talk of such delights but as yet it had come to nothing. He was the only boy in his year whose home wasn't geared to Microsoft. It put him, he felt, at a disadvantage. 'Let's try this,' he said taking out a disk without a label.

'Let me do it.'

Henry passed Jamie the disk. 'Go on then. Which way round?'

'This way.'

'No. The silver bit in first.'

Jamie pushed it in and received a satisfying clunk.

'Now what you do to read it is this.' Henry grew in

confidence and absorption. Neither of them heard Stephany and Theodora coming in from the living room.

'Hello. What are you two up to?'

'Just experimenting,' said Henry. He felt he was on safe ground. He was pretty sure they hadn't broken anything. And Stephany was a great one for learning from experience.

'Look,' said Theodora peering over their shoulders at the familiar words. ' "Change and decay is all I see around me". Where did this come from?'

CHAPTER TEN

Ember Day

The small flames hissed and spluttered as the rain caught them, then they returned to hide themselves in the mound of dead beech leaves. Every now and again the outer crust of leaves collapsed into white ash and scarlet flame leaped out anew. Soon the whole pile would be consumed. Theodora watched the small drama and savoured the smell of autumn like incense.

She had meant, this Tuesday morning, to resume her reading of the Newcome archive but the thought of settling to the turret room in the face of all that had happened yesterday was unbearable. Instead she had risen early, said her office and been to Eucharist in the tiny college chapel. There had not been many there. She had noticed Isaiah, Rita, Trevor and three or four others. Toby Spin had celebrated very fast. Training for the priesthood, she thought, involves living the monastic existence, concentrating utterly on spiritual development, on prayer. If we can't or won't do that, there will be no priesthood, only social workers or the ambitious egoists who fill the secular world.

We shall have no right to, because no foundation for, the leadership of the Church. She thought of Newcome and then of Conrad Duff, spoilt leaders both.

Now she stood on the edge of the south side of Bishop's House and gazed down over Esther Newcome's decayed garden. There was enough of the grandeur showing through to support the pretentions of the place. Its history, its theology, even, was exemplified in its gardens and buildings. The range of buildings, refectory and chapel, library and accommodation, linking the life of the community ought to impose a similar harmony and order on the life of students and staff, ordinands and priests. But it had not. Something had gone wrong here and down in the churchyard lay a man, a priest, unlamented, unmourned, who in his death as well as in his life had been a fount of discord.

Below, through the veil of slanting rain, she could see the village, dependent, originally, in the nineteenth century, both economically and emotionally on the college, now recreated as a dormitory for the secular rich. She could glimpse the parish church and the roof of Mrs Locke Tremble's cottage. What was that eccentric lady's part in all this? Then to her right, down the road, lay Oxford, a lodestone, a temptation for people like Duff, where Aidan and Tim Wade lodged together waiting. She turned to look back at Bishop's House and thought, there are too many unhappy people here. She thought of Richeldis and Crispin with twenty-odd years of hatred forming them, in a poisonous atmosphere of blame and anger. She thought of the staff, Brink, Spin, even Stephany, little minds stumbling after greater ones. There they were, Brink flailing around with no centre to him, Spin eagerbeavering after change at any price, Stephany seeking stability and comfort in simplicities which no religion, certainly not Christianity, ought to offer. Theodora felt the need to cleanse the place, to set it on a new and better track; but then caught herself up. What made her think she had the power, the wisdom to do that? But how else would the institution survive the Bishop's visitation, due, she remembered, tomorrow?

She recalled what Dan had said yesterday to her in the brief, tense phone conversation they'd had before she'd interviewed young Dr Spender. 'Where are you ringing from?' she'd asked him to try and slow him down, to relax him.

'I'm ringing from Tim's. He's out,' he'd added as though this might be important. She, too, felt exposed, clinging to the skimpy protection of the phone booth outside Thelma Gainley's office. Then he'd taken her through the events as far as he could recall them on the day of Conrad's death. She scribbled away making notes.

Finally she asked, 'Dan, what about the Atroxine bottle? When Conrad had his attack in the garden, did he have a bottle of the stuff on him?'

'No.'

'How do you know?'

'I remember Matt saying, "Look in his pocket".'

'Matt said that?'

'Yes.' Dan was firm. Did she believe him?

'And it wasn't there?'

'No. I told you, it was beside his bed.'

'You saw it there when you carried him up. I mean as soon as you carried him up.'

Dan paused. Then he said carefully, 'I noticed the

bottle when I got back from the chapel. Matt said we ought to have the reserved sacrament, just in case.'

Theodora phrased her last question carefully. 'How much Atroxine was in the bottle?'

'It was empty,' Dan said. And that, Theodora had to admit, had been young Dr Spender's view. She could hear Aidan at the other end of the line and the sound of a voice – was it Tim's? – in the background. 'Dan,' she said urgently, 'what do you think happened that day? What about the suicide note? Did you put it there?' There was more sound in the background. She was almost shouting.

'No. No, of course not. The obvious person is . . .' She couldn't quite hear.

'Who?'

'I said, Crispin is a meddler. He's quite capable of faking a note.'

'And having it on hand when his father had an attack? Putting it in his room before he left for Mrs Locke Tremble's?' But there was no answer. Dan had gone.

How had that letter got to Duff's dresser at the opportune moment? Matt, Dan, Richeldis, Crispin had all had the opportunity. And what about the bottle of Atroxine which Mrs Gainley had come across in Matt Brink's in tray at half past eleven in the morning? There were times when Theodora wished she had the powers of the police and could simply summon people to see her. For a moment she toyed with that broad path. Could she not just phone the local constabulary and tell them what she knew and was beginning to suspect? But she knew she was too deep in. She'd have to soldier on until she could present the entire picture.

Resigned, she drew her Barbour hood over her head and plodded through the driving rain towards Bishop's House.

Thelma Gainley's room was small and full of wet students smelling like wet dogs. Mrs Gainley was dealing rapidly with inquiries about delays in grant payments for first years, requests for Ordinance Survey maps and whether there was anywhere nearer than Oxford to buy stationery. 'I haven't got a Biro to bless myself with,' said one plaintive, dripping figure.

'Here, take this,' said Mrs Gainley kindly, 'to tide you over.'

Theodora was reminded of that rare breed of copers, the school secretary. Any minute now someone would come in with a grazed knee asking for a plaster and an aspirin. But as the chapel clock struck ten the wet ones melted away to classes.

Mrs Gainley turned to Theodora. 'Just as well Matt had his barbeque yesterday. We'd have been drowned out in this.'

'Very wet, the Chilterns,' Theodora agreed. 'Always were. Something to do with the beech leaves dripping on to you. Have you got a minute?'

'Yes,' said Mrs Gainley, as though she might have been waiting for her. 'Half a mo.' She produced a white handwritten card which said 'Temporarily Closed' in neat italics, opened her door and slid it into the brass holder.

Theodora liked the 'Temporarily'.

'Don't want to be unavailable but you've got to protect your privacy sometimes to get any work done at all. Now.' She swivelled her chair towards Theodora who propped herself on the low counter which separated the files and computers from the customers. 'Now, it'll be about Conrad.'

Theodora nodded.

'You made any progress?'

'A bit. For example, I saw Dr Spender yesterday.'

'Not the man his father was.'

'In what way?'

'Cuts corners.'

'Which ones?'

'Patients ask and he gives.'

'Atroxine?'

'Doled out like sweeties.'

'How do you know?'

Mrs Gainley ruminated. Surely she wasn't going to nap now? Finally she said, 'Crispin.'

'Said what, when?'

'Oh, it was a week or two before Conrad died. He used to drift over here when he'd nothing better to do and talk about his dramatic ambitions. A bit of fairly harmless fantasy as far as Crispin was concerned. Well, anyway, he'd come over. He'd had a row with his dad and more unusually, with Richeldis. He said something like "He'll never die if she keeps fussing over his medicine." And I said, "What medicine?" and he said, "Well, she's got him some more of his stuff from Spender."'

'Did he say why?'

'Said she said they might need more if they went on holiday.'

'Were they planning to?'

'Haven't taken a holiday together for years. Conrad sometimes took a weekend fishing with Wade in the Dales but never with Richeldis or Crispin. Most unconvincing reason. Old Spender would have known that, smelt a rat.'

'What sort of a rat? I mean, why do you think she wanted more Atroxine?' Theodora could feel the tension mounting within herself, within Mrs Gainley, too.

'It did occur to me that if he got too much of the stuff inside himself . . .'

'He'd die,' Theodora finished as Mrs Gainley hesitated. 'Did she plan that? Did she execute that?'

Mrs Gainley shook her head. She didn't look at Theodora.

'Look,' said Theodora. After all, she had to trust someone. 'Dan rang me yesterday and told me all he could remember about the day of Conrad's death. He said he'd been over the events. He'd tried to picture things in Conrad's room when they brought him up from the garden. He said when they got him on to the bed, Brink had put Conrad's jacket over the chair beside the bed. Then Richeldis had come in and they'd had a barney about sending for the doctor. Richeldis said not until Crispin comes. When asked why not Richeldis said she wanted Crispin to see his father dying. "There is a beginning of suffering and there is an end of suffering," she said. Brink said, well, where is he? And Richeldis said she knew where he was. He wouldn't be long. After that she went out and Dan heard her phoning from downstairs.'

'Then what?'

'Then Dan said Brink sent him for the reserved sacrament.'

'At what point did Dan notice that there was an Atroxine bottle beside the bed?'

'When he returned and just before Spender arrived.'

Mrs Gainley thought about this. 'What you're saying is that neither Dan nor Brink could have known that there was an extra Atroxine bottle in the house.'

Theodora agreed. 'Only Crispin would know that his mother had ordered more Atroxine.'

'So Richeldis . . .' Mrs Gainley didn't finish.

'Or perhaps Crispin?' Theodora asked.

'But he was out of the house. Unless he put it there before and Dan didn't notice it until later.'

'But it could have been Richeldis.'

'How about the extra bottle in Brink's in tray?'

'A little incriminating present from Richeldis?'

'Or Richeldis via Crispin?'

'Or Crispin via Richeldis.'

The rain had ceased over lunch time. A grey mist-like steam had risen from the summer-warmed earth. Every shrub carried its charge of water. Footprints across the grass in front of the Warden's garden entrance left dark tracks. Theodora, making her way towards the French windows (she had eschewed the pantomime of knocking fruitlessly at the front door of the lodgings), could trace one other set of footsteps before her own. Would that be Richeldis or Crispin or someone else?

She reached the windows and tapped on the pane. There was no movement within the house. She cupped her hand to the glass but could see nothing. She tried the handle and the door swung open. Theodora stepped inside and stopped.

The room which had been so crowded with furniture was bare. The carpet lay rolled up in one corner. The mantelshelf had been stripped of clock and candles.

Where the piano had been a single sheet of music lingered. Dark patches on the walls marked the absence of pictures. Cautiously Theodora stepped across the grey boards to the door.

'Hello,' she called, honour bound. There was no response. She crossed the hall with the staircase leading to the bedrooms and the turret room which had become so familiar to her. There was a door into the dining room which she had never seen and beyond that a door to the kitchen. After a moment's hesitation she opened the dining-room door. It was larger than she'd imagined. The smeared table would have seated ten. The room smelt of boiled cabbage. Here, too, there was signs of removal. Tea chests of china and books stood round the sides of the room. Chairs had been stacked seat to seat. On one corner of the table were a pile of books and papers, and a mug and crumby plate. At the other end a copy of *The Times* with the crossword half done. Theodora immediately assigned the first pile to Crispin, *The Times* pile to Richeldis. It was the piece of paper which lay between the two that caught her eye. There it was again, 'Change and decay is all I see . . .' So Crispin had a copy of the suicide note? Or was it Richeldis? Theodora considered the position of the paper. It really did lie exactly between the two piles. Had one passed it to the other? And who had passed it to whom? Then she thought perhaps it was the letter itself, the one Conrad had had on his dresser. But no, that one would have had creases in; it had been folded, according to Richeldis. This one, on the contrary, had never been folded. She was strongly tempted to lift the page when she became aware of voices. At the end of the room was a hatch.

Having embarked on a life of crime, Theodora thought, I may as well continue. She moved across the room but before she reached the hatch, the flap flew up and Theodora found herself face to face with Richeldis.

Theodora gazed into the latter's eye at far too close a range for comfort.

'What are you doing in my dining room?'

It was the sort of question the honourable have nightmares about being asked. 'Why did you tell me your husband died of an absence of Atroxine when you knew very well he'd got another bottle in the house?' Theodora countered.

The flap of the hatch came down between them like a guillotine. Theodora moved swiftly for the door, raced down the corridor and flung open the kitchen door. Richeldis was standing by the other side of the hatch. A cool breeze blew from the open back door and Theodora glimpsed the scantily clad figure of Crispin running down the path.

'Would you care for some coffee?' Richeldis's tone was that of the normal hostess. There was no indication of the oddity of the situation, the earnest of violence in the slamming of the hatch door, the anger and directness of Theodora's question.

'As you see,' Richeldis went on, 'we are in the throes of moving. My son and I intend to start a new life. I have always wanted to live in London. What do you think?'

Theodora ignored the coffee question. 'You asked me, no, forced me, to inquire into the circumstances of your husband's death.'

Richeldis smiled. 'So I did. I want Crispin to start his new life free of guilty encumbrances.'

'You haven't answered my question about the Atroxine. You knew there was an extra bottle of Atroxine in the house but you persisted in telling me that Conrad died of a lack of it.'

'I'm afraid I don't follow you.' Richeldis's tone was quite level, the emotion either genuine or well under control.

'When they, when Dan and Matt brought Conrad upstairs from the garden, you asked about the Atroxine in his jacket pocket.

'True, and poor Matt couldn't find any. So he said.' Richeldis's tone was scoffing.

'You mean you doubt it?'

'No, no, by then Matt had taken it.' Richeldis was madly complacent. Theodora saw she'd got it all worked out.

'Matt Brink had deprived Conrad of the Atroxine?'

'Or Dan Prior of course. It could have been either really.'

'How do you know it hadn't disappeared earlier? How do you know Crispin hadn't taken it when he quarrelled with Conrad before lunch?'

'You could never prove it.'

'Crispin has a copy of the suicide note made up of scraps of the draft of some material which Dan Prior had prepared for Conrad.'

'I would rather say that Prior has the original and used it. Anything my son has is merely derived from it. Possibly Aidan gave it to him.'

Why did Theodora feel this was all a mad inversion, a mirror image of reality? Was it simply that she did not care for Crispin and did care for Dan, did therefore want the one to be guilty and the other to be innocent?

Richeldis looked round the disordered room as though she had lost interest in the conversation. Theodora was filled with a wish to make her face reality.

'Mrs Duff,' she began, 'you asked me to find out who was responsible for your husband's death. My view is that there is increasingly strong evidence that your son was responsible.'

Richeldis turned away from her and began to busy herself wrapping china in back copies of the *Church Times*. 'Nonsense,' she said firmly. 'Crispin wouldn't kill his father unless I told him to. I am the only person who loves Crispin. Many do not find him lovable. He depends on me. Unless I gave him the word, he wouldn't do it.'

Theodora did not know whether to laugh or cry. The cold-bloodedness of it all. Was this the reason this crazy woman had set her on in the first place? Was Richeldis merely piqued that someone had pipped her to the post in killing her husband and she had determined that that person was not going to be her son?

'And you didn't tell him to?' Theodora thought she might as well get an answer.

'No.'

'You had other plans?'

Richeldis smiled. 'If you mean did I intend to kill him myself, Miss Braithwaite, the answer, as I'm sure you're aware, is yes. Only someone forestalled me.'

CHAPTER ELEVEN

Church and World

The Bishop's car was crowded. The chauffeur was a big man; the Bishop was a tall one; his Archdeacon filled his space solidly. The Bishop also carried a crook. He had a large collection of crooks all propped up round the walls of his drawing room. Just in case, said some of his clergy, a lost sheep should wander past and need to be drawn in. This particular crook took to pieces for easy stowage but without his chaplain the Bishop wasn't sure how to assemble it so he'd thought it best to come with it done. It kept poking the Archdeacon.

The Bishop had a kind face and a forgiving smile. He forgave people before they were aware they needed forgiving. This often made them feel guilty. He was not looking forward to his day. Gracemount had a long and honourable history. It had produced six bishops that he could remember and probably more he couldn't. Its Wardens after Newcome had all been men of modest distinction. Some, like Conrad Duff, had been men to be reckoned with, their networks as wide in politics and academia as in the Church.

But the order had come down from the very top. 'Cut, cut, cut.' He'd felt strongly enough to voice a dissenting view. 'Human resources, the most important of the Church's assets; proper training one of its first duties.' The Archbishop had had to put him right on that one, Peter. He hadn't quite been told that the Church's most important assets lay in the shopping malls of Macclesfield and the hands of Kleinwort Benson. But he could sense the unspoken. 'No point,' the boss had said, 'in training more full-time priests we can't pay or pension. The future,' the Archbishop had said with his wide, generous, open look, 'lies with the NSM and the ladies, God bless them. They're quite used to doing two jobs and working for peanuts. That's true Christian ministry, a lesson to us all,' he'd said as he leaned back in his full-time chair. 'A whole new model.' He'd learnt the word on his last management course. 'And, you know,' the Archbishop had leaned closer so that the Bishop could see his tombstone teeth, 'there's less and less place in the modern Church for hothouses like Gracemount. Priests need to be trained where they'll work, on the job, in the front line, at the coal face, amongst the grass roots. The inner cities.' He used the sacred term with reverence. 'In our factories and shops, in our offices and . . .' The Bishop had switched off. The litany was familiar to him. It silenced without convincing him. 'We've got to set an example to the world of good management,' the Archbishop had changed his diction to old speak, 'of good *stewardship.*' The Bishop had just enough wordliness to know that whatever it was the Church could teach the world, it wasn't good management.

'Anyway,' the Archbishop had concluded, 'there's

something unhealthy about Gracemount. Conrad Duff,'
he sought the word from his none too extensive vocabulary, 'wasn't straight.' And there the Bishop had to
admit that he might have a point.

The clock was striking half past nine as the new
Rover (buy British) crunched the weedy gravel outside
Bishop's House. Thelma Gainley reached for her
internal phone first for Brink's office, then to the library
for Spin. The latter rarely spent much time in the
librarian's cubbyhole but in the light of the visit he
had felt it was an appropriate place to be called from.
Finally, she rang Stephany at home. To each she said,
'He's here.'

'Where's Richeldis?' Brink had asked Mrs Gainley.

'Gone to the village. Visiting Maria Locke Tremble.'

'And Crispin?'

'Gone into Oxford on the bus. I told him the Bishop's
party wasn't due till three.'

'Thank Heaven,' Brink said. 'With any luck they'll
be gone by then.' With a lighter heart he sped across
the hall to meet his guests.

Observers unused to the modern manners of the
Anglican Church might have been surprised at the
warmth of the greetings usual between clergy. Men
who hardly knew each other would clasp each other
warmly by the hand and call each other by first names,
as though this very act guaranteed brotherhood and
fellow feeling. Theodora, passing through the hall on
the way to the library, heard the familiar heartiness
which always reminded her of Kipling's description
of male camaraderie, 'the deep-voiced laughter of men'.

The Bishop was introducing his Archdeacon. The
Archdeacon had a limp and a cast in one eye. He was

known in the diocese as Jolly Roger. He never smiled. He knew all there was to know about his job, including the fact that he'd never make the Bishops' bench. He cherished no vestige of charity and he did all the Bishop's administrative work, including the dirty bits. The Bishop, if questioned, would have said that the Venerable Roger Pyke's qualities complemented his own. This was Bishop's speak for 'I can't stand him but he's very useful'.

Theodora had nearly reached the corridor when the Bishop, looking up from being affable to Spin, caught sight of her.

'Theo. Theodora. Miss Braithwaite,' he exclaimed with real pleasure. 'I'd no idea you were on the staff here.'

Theodora couldn't do otherwise than make herself agreeable. 'Good morning, Bishop,' she said, ignoring his informality. 'I'm not.'

'Theo's making use of our archive,' said Spin. He was, after all, librarian.

'A life of our founder, Thomas Henry Newcome,' Brink contributed. Theodora's stock went up. If she knew the Bishop, there was no telling who else she might know.

'Ah,' said the Bishop, 'a mighty figure. Just what we could do with to raise our spirits at the present juncture. I wish I had time to do some reading. How are you getting on?'

'Slowly,' said Theodora cautiously.

'Well, carry on with the good work. You'll be joining us for lunch, I hope. I could do with some elevating conversation.' He looked at Spin, Brink and the Archdeacon.

'Twelve thirty for one. Sherry in my room, if you'd care to look in,' said Brink, sizing matters up. What the Bishop wanted, the Bishop should have, in this at least.

The table in Brink's room looked unaccustomedly clear. He, the Bishop and the Archdeacon took their seats.

'Shall we begin with prayer?'

'And now,' said the Bishop when he'd finished commending things to Almighty God, 'I'll hand over to Roger here to guide us through the agenda.'

The Archdeacon put his papers exactly on top of one another and swivelled his good eye round to Brink. 'The future of the college,' he began.

'Dan,' Theodora was urgent, 'I have to see you.' The telephone outside Mrs Gainley's office seemed terribly exposed. 'About Conrad's death.' She felt as though she were addressing the entire college. 'No, I can't. I've been invited to lunch with the Bishop. There's no way I can get into Oxford and back in time. You'll have to come out.'

She could hear him ducking and weaving. How low in the world this golden boy had sunk.

'Well, if you feel like that, we could meet in the grounds. How about the Hermes pond? The round one in the woods.'

And shortly before eleven, he was there, lounging against the silver bark of a beech in the pose of Hilliard's miniature.

'Henry found Duff's suicide note on one of your PC disks.' She waited. Dan gazed across at where Hermes should be as though he could do with that messenger from the pagan gods to help him. Finally, he said, 'What suicide note?'

'There was a single piece of A4 on Conrad's dresser while he lay dying. Brink read it. Richeldis took it. It contained the line "change and decay I see all around".'

There was a pause, then Dan said, 'It was part of his work on *The Darkened Glass*. Part of the stuff I was helping him with. I did the drafting. I told you.' He sounded pettish like a child making excuses.

'So how did that portion of it, just those sentences, get into a letter on Conrad Duff's dresser hours or was it minutes before his death?'

'Look, I gave him that stuff weeks ago. I don't know how it got to his dresser. He might have put it there himself. Or perhaps someone else got hold of it and put it there.'

'So the stuff you took over the morning of his death wasn't the stuff in the so-called suicide note?'

'No. It wasn't.' Aidan was firm. 'What I took over that morning was a translation of some quotations from Clement of Alexandria. I told you, my Greek's better than Conrad's.'

'So the suicide stuff had been about for some time.'

'Yes. Look, why is it important?'

'Could someone have doctored your earlier stuff to turn it into a suicide note?'

Dan thought for a moment. 'Might they, I mean Matt and Richeldis, just have mistaken the page for a note? Was it addressed to anyone?'

Theodora tried to recall the crumpled piece of paper which Richeldis had shown her.

'There was nothing on the back of it. I'm pretty sure.'

'So it could just have been turned into a suicide note in Matt's and Rick's imagination.'

'What would prompt them to think that?'

'Was death in their minds?'

For a moment Theodora wondered if Richeldis and Matthew Brink had colluded in Conrad's death. 'If it wasn't a suicide note, just a stray page from *The Darkened Glass*, how might it have got on to Conrad's dresser?'

'My first thought would be Crispin.'

'But?'

'All this shouting about "I killed my father" made me think not.'

'So?'

'What about Richeldis?' Dan sounded as though he was suggesting rather than accusing. As though if he offered Theodora something, she might leave him alone.

'It would only make sense if she intended to kill him and make it look like suicide.' Theodora pointed out. 'But in fact she didn't let the note leave the bedroom, did she? She told me that she took it out of Brink's hands.'

'What are you saying?' Dan sounded tired to death.

'So it was either you or Brink or Richeldis or Crispin.'

She considered how much she was prepared to tell Aidan. How much did she believe him when he said he could never kill Duff? She experimented. 'How do you think he died?'

'Heart attack, initially, I've no doubt of that but I had thought, as I told you, that he'd got rid of his Atroxine himself.' Dan was definite.

'The bottle wasn't in his pocket, you mean?'

'I told you, it was beside his bed.'

'He didn't get a chance to get to it. He was overtaken in the garden.' Theodora pressed on. 'Dan, did you know Duff had been asked to do the Crockford preface?'

Dan considered. 'Yes.'

'When and how did you find out?'

'Conrad told me, about three months ago.'

'Did he tell you what he was going to do?'

'It was going to be a shortened version of the thesis of *The Darkened Glass*.'

'Richeldis thinks he had a rather different plan.' Theodora told him Richeldis's version.

'They'd never publish.'

'They might. It depends a bit on how it was phrased. After all, it's a burning issue in the Church of England. It might well produce another split, like the women priests thing, and that would finish it. It's an area in which feelings in the Church run high. And even if they didn't use it, if Duff made it known that he had that knowledge and was prepared to publish it in some form, wouldn't that have made him a . . . a target?'

'Who would care enough about the Church to want to stop him doing that?'

'Would you, Aidan?' Theodora asked gently.

The morning went from bad to worse. The Bishop and Archdeacon wanted to meet and interview separately all the staff. Then they wanted to meet 'a representative sample of the students'.

'What on earth would that look like?' Brink had taken the excuse of organising coffee to consult Mrs Gainley.

'One woman, one black, one working class,' she had

replied, wiser in the ways of the politically correct world than Brink.

'Which would give you an unrepresentative sample,' Stephany, marking time in the bursar's office before her interview, had pointed out. 'The majority are white middle-class males.'

'Just leave it to me.' Mrs Gainley scrolled down on the computer screen the names Isaiah Ngaio, Trevor Fisher and Rita Nougatt.

'Do you think they've really come to learn, or is it just a face-saving exercise?' Toby Spin, fresh from his session, inquired.

'Senior clerics' idea of consultation is to make up their minds what they're going to do and then invite the victims to agree with them.' Mrs Gainley was wiser in the ways of the Church than any of them too.

'Or failing that, they fix it in car parks.' Spin was bitter.

'Then they wonder why no one trusts their systems.' Stephany had the sociologist's view.

'I think if we can show them that work of real quality is going on here, both amongst the students and the staff, we can make a good case for continuing.' Brink felt leadership required optimism.

By twelve the Bishop and the Archdeacon had seen all the staff. Brink had said, 'Of course, we shall need a leader, a new Warden of real quality, of energy, resource, and distinction to carry on our marvellous tradition here faithfully. I think optimism is the prime quality I should be looking for.' The Bishop had looked at him thoughtfully and nodded.

When they had called Spin he'd said, 'We need to market the place. Keep it in the public eye. New and innovative courses. Myers Briggs groups. Experiential liturgy. A leven of creation theology.' The Bishop had shuddered. 'Host a conference for DDOs and show them what their candidates would get,' Spin had imprudently concluded.

Stephany had said, 'The social structures and directing values of the twenty-first century will be entirely different from those of the twentieth. The age of postmodernism is upon us. What *is* the vision, what *are* the new structures which the Church will need if it is to cope with change and survive? Where is that thinking going on?' The Bishop and the Archdeacon had concluded swiftly with belittling thanks.

'How about lunch?' said the Bishop hungrily. 'Listening to people always gives me an appetite.'

Brink led him across to his drawing room. Theodora, entering five minutes later, heard Brink saying desperately, 'But we're training priests. Tranquillity, a certain withdrawal from the pressures of the world, a chance to establish a proper spiritual discipline in one's own life is terribly necessary, is part of our tradition.'

The Bishop remembered the Archbishop and curbed his agreement. He marked Theodora's appearance with relief.

Theodora looked across the room. She felt drained of energy and hope. She would have to take steps, explain and inform. She wished she'd never come to Gracemount. She noticed that they'd got together what they took, doubtless, to be a representative sample of the college's intake. Isaiah Ngaio was being interrogated by the Bishop. Rita had been taken on by the Archdeacon. Trevor was drinking sherry with distaste with Spin. Brink was telling Stephany what he had told the Bishop and

Archdeacon twenty minutes ago. Mrs Gainley was refilling a tray of glasses. The room was small and the October sun hot. The window stood open.

'Here,' said Mrs Gainley, 'have a big one. You look as though you've been working too hard.' There was something conspiratorial about Mrs Gainley. She clearly regarded Theodora as a chum.

'How's Hovis?' Theodora dutifully inquired.

'His offside hind . . .' Mrs Gainley began and froze. She edged past Theodora to the window and then whispered, 'Richeldis Duff's just come up the drive.'

Theodora learned against the glass pane and glimpsed Richeldis dismounting from an upright bicycle and disappearing through the wicket gate in the yew hedge into the Warden's garden.

'I had hoped she wouldn't be back until after the Bishop's party had left. I told the Bishop she wasn't in. He'll naturally want to say a word – of comfort,' she added by way of explanation.

'I expect she's seen his car,' Theodora said. 'And I saw Crispin ten minutes ago running through the woods by the Hermes pond.'

'Ah well, the best laid plans of mice and men,' said Mrs Gainley. 'I did what I could. We're in the hands of Providence. Crispin won't be able to . . .'

But whatever it was Mrs Gainley thought Crispin would not be able to do was lost as the door opened and Crispin himself, complete with running kit, entered.

'I want everyone to know,' he said clearly and apparently calmly, 'that I killed my father.'

'No,' said Theodora wearily from beside the window. 'No, you did not.'

* * *

Isaiah spread out the papers on the floor of Trevor's sitting room. Theodora, Rita, and Trevor watched.

'If they contain what you say they contain,' Rita looked at Theodora, 'couldn't we burn them?'

It was a strong temptation. Why should the Church's reputation be harmed yet again by the hypocrisy of its senior members? But then hadn't just that very motive, the desire to protect the Church, led to murder? 'I'm afraid they're an important piece of evidence,' Theodora said. 'They show the state of mind of Conrad Duff and also just why someone might try to prevent what he was writing coming to light. The police will want them.' She glanced at Isaiah.

'If it serves justice,' he said, 'then they must have them. I think your police are not like ours. They do not take bribes.'

'Only in certain cases,' said Rita to keep the record straight.

'Well, they're not complete, I have used some for kindling.' Isaiah looked with regret at the rest and felt the waste.

'Where were they?' Trevor recognised that his role was probably going to be to feed the questions. Anyway, he genuinely wanted to know what was going on. He'd got a four pack of draught Guinness on with Rita about who'd done what, so he had a material interest.

'They're notes from his father's draft of a preface for the new edition of Crockford.'

'He nicked them?' Rita reckoned she could tell a thief.

'Yes. He took them the night before his father died and hid them, as he thought, in the chimney of my room.'

'But in fact they were in my chimney.' Light dawned on Isaiah.

'The rooms are on the same corridor and are very alike. In a hurry it's easy to mistake them,' Theodora agreed.

'What on earth did he expect to do with them?' Trevor could not conceive any set of notes being valuable.

'He had certain needs. He wanted out, a place of his own and a career in acting which would take him to London.'

'And he was going to blackmail his dad to get that?' Rita asked. 'But surely Conrad could easily rehash his notes even if it took him time?'

'The point about the Crockford preface is that it's supposed to be anonymous. If Crispin released the name of the writer, especially if he did so at a moment of his own choosing, he might have a lever on his father,' Theodora pointed out. 'Anyway, I don't suppose Crispin thought about it too clearly. He saw a chance and took it.'

'But his dad found out?' Trevor was quite interested now. He wanted a story.

'Yes.'

' "The wages of sin are death",' said Isaiah sombrely.

'So Crispin thought. When Conrad found his stuff was missing about half past ten on the morning of the eighth of September, he summoned Crispin and there was a row. That was the quarrel which Richeldis heard and which later Crispin told Mrs Locke Tremble about. Crispin genuinely thought that his row had precipitated his father's heart attack and contributed to his father's death.'

'So he did . . .' Trevor began.

Theodora cut him short. 'Conrad did absolutely everything which would entitle him to think he'd killed his father. He pilferred his notes and precipitated a row. He took his Atroxine from his father's jacket pocket and so deprived him of it if he should have an attack. He placed a sheet of the Crockford notes on his dresser to give the impression it might be a suicide note. Then, for good measure, he put the Atroxine bottle he'd taken from his father in Brink's in tray where it was seen by Mrs Gainley.'

'Why?' Trevor asked.

'Spite,' said Rita before Theodora could answer. 'He's spiteful is that lad.'

'Yes,' Theodora agreed. 'But still Crispin *didn't* kill his father. Conrad died of an overdose of Atroxine, not a lack of it, and with that fact Crispin had nothing to do.'

'How do you know?'

Theodora spoke of Dr Spender.

'Hey, I knew Richeldis had done it. I told you so.'

Rita found Trevor's outburst tasteless. She looked at Theodora speculatively. 'Who knew about the preface and who cared enough to kill to prevent its publication?' she asked shrewdly.

'Richeldis did have a part. She got together enough of the Atroxine to have a lethal dose on hand.'

'But didn't use it?'

'No. She may have intended to. She certainly heard the row and perhaps knew enough about her husband's state of health to guess that he might have an attack. But when he did have one she wasn't on hand.'

'So who was?' Rita pressed on.

'Dan was there,' Trevor said slowly. 'He told me.'
He looked at Theodora. 'He's a really nice bloke, is
Dan. Plays a good game of hockey. I wouldn't like to
think . . .'

'Dan came round at about ten with some papers
for Conrad's book *The Darkened Glass*. Conrad told
Dan to come back after lunch to discuss the translation.
At two he did come back and this time Brink was with
him. They found Conrad in the throes of an attack.
They carried him up to his bedroom and . . .'

'Someone gave him more Atroxine than was good
for him,' Rita finished.

'Who?' Trevor leaned forward.

'Either Mr Brink or Aidan,' said Isaiah. He wondered
if he had at last grasped the analytical technique.

'They were both alone with him in his bedroom.
Either of them could have pushed more Atroxine into
him to deliver the *coup de grâce*. Either of them might
have felt that rather than the Church having to face
another row which might besmirch many good men
as well as many not so good it would be better for
Conrad Duff to die.'

'But only one of them did.'

'One of them left to get the reserved sacrament from
the chapel. The other fed Duff the lethal dose of
Atroxine.'

POST MORTEM

The organ, lavishly ornate in its accompaniment of 'The Church's one foundation' under the hand of Mrs Locke Tremble, died away. Verse three had been omitted; 'by schism rent asunder, by heresies distressed' seemed too near the mark for the remaining senior members of St Sylvester's Gracemount.

The preacher, who had left it a bit late, paced towards the pulpit and mounted in dead silence.

'In the name of the . . .' Trevor began uncertainly. In the second row Toby Spin raised his right hand slightly towards the roof. Trevor cleared his throat, raised his eyes and bounced it off the corbel.

'The Church has different needs at different times,' he began unexceptionally. The congregation of ordinands, tutors, parents, husbands, wives and the odd parishioner at this half-term service settled back to be bored. Only Isaiah Ngaio out of a genuine wish to learn and Rita out of loyalty to her man looked alert. Theodora, in the back row, wondered if anyone should be allowed to preach before the age of fifty. What could

211

they have to say before they'd had time to reflect maturely on their experience? No wonder so many of them resorted to ill-judged chumminess and personal anecdote. Though, she conceded, of course the Spirit could use any vehicle. She looked up at the halting Trevor beneath whose surplice could be seen the green pullover which was his defence against the suddenly cold weather at the end of October.

'And the Church's need at the present time is to educate, firstly itself and then the world. We need to realise that the whole of creation has been set up as one giant classroom, everything that happens to us is there to teach us some lesson or other.'

Trevor's mum in the second row thought what a clever boy their Trev had turned out and what a pity it was that he wanted to throw it all away on the Church. Now Chapel she could have understood. Still, her pully looked nice on him.

In the choir stalls Stephany and Aidan on opposite benches faced each other. Each thought of what the recent past had taught them. Stephany thought, marriage is for life as far as she was concerned. Whatever Dan had done, it wasn't going to ruin them. We'll work at it. We'll pray together. We'll put down new and different foundations. Above all, Jamie and Henry must not suffer.

Aidan thought how much, perversely, he missed Conrad Duff. His intelligence, his irony, his range of reading, his ascerbity and worldliness were a tonic he ached for. He thought what a narrow shave he'd had. His luck had held. He had a clean bill of health from Dr Spender. Poor Brink. He'd loved Conrad too but in the end he'd valued the institution of the Church more. He looked down the nave to where Tim Wade sat expressionless, appraising, giving nothing away. Well, Dan thought, if he couldn't be a priest he'd make an effort to be good at something else. In the past, being good at things had been easy. Perhaps with Stephany's help, with God's, it might come again. Tim Wade had said he might just be able to get him into a junior teaching post at York where, he understood, they offered a Classical Literature in Translation course. The network ought to work for him.

Theodora looked across at Aidan and thought of Brink. What, she wondered, would happen now? She'd arranged the evidence and put it to the Bishop. She had watched his face as he wrestled with the Anglican senior clergy's natural inclination to do nothing, to hush it up, to deny its existence. 'You see,' Theodora pointed out, 'one of the two of them, Aidan Prior and Matthew Brink, both knew Conrad had been asked to write the Crockford preface. But Aidan thought the content was going to be a shortened version of Conrad's book *The Darkened Glass*. Only Brink knew Conrad intended to use scandalous information which would harm the Church. The Bishop had resisted the temptation to call the Archdeacon. 'All right,' he said at last. 'I'll see to it.'

'The only way the Church can teach the world,' Trevor was coming up to his finishing post and increased his speed accordingly, 'is by doing, by living the Gospel out, by setting an example in every part of our lives.'

Would Gracemount have a place in the future Church of England? Theodora admitted it seemed unlikely. Her mind went back to something she had read in one of Esther Newcome's letters. 'I am resolved we shall have a new beginning.' Well, Theodora reckoned she'd have to do that herself. The very least she owed the truth was to do a joint biography of Thomas Henry and Esther. It would make for a better balance. He the thinker, she the doer, if that was how it was. She thought of Conrad Duff compared with Thomas Henry Newcome and Richeldis compared with Esther. Really, the Victorians had more stamina.

'It's no good preaching,' Trevor was concluding with distaste. 'It's no good being clever scholars. It's no good *telling* the world what to do or how to vote. We've got too many beams in our own eyes to do that. We, every man jack of us, have got to *show* how. We're the demonstration models. All of us.'

A selection of bestsellers from Headline

ASKING FOR TROUBLE	Ann Granger	£5.99 ☐
FAITHFUL UNTO DEATH	Caroline Graham	£5.99 ☐
THE WICKED WINTER	Kate Sedley	£5.99 ☐
HOTEL PARADISE	Martha Grimes	£5.99 ☐
MURDER IN THE MOTORSTABLE	Amy Myers	£5.99 ☐
WEIGHED IN THE BALANCE	Anne Perry	£5.99 ☐
THE DEVIL'S HUNT	P C Doherty	£5.99 ☐
EVERY DEADLY SIN	D M Greenwood	£4.99 ☐
SKINNER'S ORDEAL	Quintin Jardine	£5.99 ☐
HONKY TONK KAT	Karen Kijewski	£5.99 ☐
THE QUICK AND THE DEAD	Alison Joseph	£5.99 ☐
THE RELIC MURDERS	Michael Clynes	£5.99 ☐

All Headline books are available at your local bookshop or newsagent, or can be ordered direct from the publisher. Just tick the titles you want and fill in the form below. Prices and availability subject to change without notice.

Headline Book Publishing, Cash Sales Department, Bookpoint, 39 Milton Park, Abingdon, OXON, OX14 4TD, UK. If you have a credit card you may order by telephone – 01235 400400.

Please enclose a cheque or postal order made payable to Bookpoint Ltd to the value of the cover price and allow the following for postage and packing:

UK & BFPO: £1.00 for the first book, 50p for the second book and 30p for each additional book ordered up to a maximum charge of £3.00.

OVERSEAS & EIRE: £2.00 for the first book, £1.00 for the second book and 50p for each additional book.

Name ....

Address ....

....

....

If you would prefer to pay by credit card, please complete:
Please debit my Visa/Access/Diner's Card/American Express (delete as applicable) card no:

Signature .... Expiry Date ....